Short story 1 # Mirror, mirror on the wall

Chapter 1:

"Mirror, mirror on the wall, who is the fairest one of all," Daphne said looking in her small mirror she kept in her bedroom. "Did you know that in the Disney movie they said: Magic mirror and not mirror mirror," she continued turning around looking at her best friend Danny.
He shook his head. "Nobody cares about that kind of stuff…"
"I do…people should always try to have their useless facts correct! Just wait till I tell you about the Droste Effect" she jokingly said. They got up and went downstairs coming across Daphne's mother on their way out.
"We'll be back at 11 pm tonight, it's the last rehearsal!" Daphne half shouted towards her mother opening the door.
"Okay, have fun dears!" she replied. Daphne and Danny walked to the high school where they would rehearse in the gym.
As part of the Drama club they got to perform a play at least once a year. This year the school decided to do Snow White and the seven dwarfs. Not the Disney version but a more serious version from the original tales of the Grimm brothers. After all, this wasn't kindergarten. Daphne was playing the evil Queen. A role she absolutely loved. She was driving Danny crazy with her evil laughter. Danny played the huntsman. A small but important role as he said. They arrived at the gym and went in. Their coach Mrs Brown was just preparing some things on stage one of which was a new magic mirror which they hadn't used before. Mrs Brown waved them forward.
"Hello there! Look at what I found yesterday!" she exclaimed. "It's a mirror specifically made for this story. See, we can play

the recorded bits of the "Mirror" and they will show up on the mirror," to prove her point she did something on her laptop and the video of Rory, who played the Mirror showed up in the middle.

"My Queen, you are the fairest one of all." His deep voice said.

"That is so cool Mrs Brown!" Danny said. He walked to the mirror and looked into it. "And it works like a normal mirror when the video is not playing too! Imagine how you can fool your friends with a mirror like this!" He touched the frame of the mirror and jumped backwards

"Oowww!"

"What happened?" Daphne asked slightly worried.

"Nothing...I guess I got a static shock...although it hurts quite a bit," Danny said.

Mrs Brown looked at him. "Hmmm, yes I guess the frame is made out of metal, actually it's quite old already, not the display but the frame itself, from the 60's or so, Daphne, you better not touch the frame," she said unconcerned. "Now, time to get dressed. Come on, we have a show to do!"

The rehearsal went great and Mrs Brown was handing out compliments to everyone.

"Great job everyone, now...be here tomorrow at 4 pm so we can start with make-up and hair so we are ready to start the play at 8 pm! Rest and take an extra look at your lines..." her phone started ringing and she looked at it. "Oooh, I'm going to have to take this, see you tomorrow!" Mrs Brown walked of stage to the dressing room and disappeared from sight. The other actors also left quickly so Daphne and Danny where the only ones who stayed behind. Daphne rolled the clear 'glass' coffin from the stage. Danny stood in front of the mirror transfixed as in a daze. Daphne turned around and walked towards him.

"Dan…" she said. He didn't respond.

"Dan…can you hear me?" she said. He still didn't respond. She stood next to him and poked him in his side.

"Dan!" she shouted.

"What?!" he said annoyed getting out of the way from her finger poking his side.

"What do you mean, what?! You were staring at your reflection as if you were hypnotized," she said incredulous. He seemed to consider this in his mind but then gave a big grin.

"Ha, fooled you!" he said. Daphne looked at him and then started laughing too.

"Wow…and I thought…my jokes were bad," she said. They cleaned up the rest of the stage so it was ready for the tomorrow's big show. Danny said good bye to Daphne when they exited the school and he went towards home, a couple of streets away from where Daphne lived.

Chapter 2:

Danny opened the door. It was dark in the house, he guessed his parents and little brother already went to sleep. It was around midnight after all. He quickly and silently went upstairs and prepared for going to bed. He showered, put on his pajamas and stood in front of the mirror to brush his teeth.

"What are you standing there for!" he suddenly heard. He looked to his left to see his little brother standing in the door.

"I'm…I'm brushing my teeth…" he said spitting the water out of his mouth. What do you think I'm doing?"

"At three in the morning?" his brother replied. "You're weird… and if you're finished can you please leave…I need to pee," Danny looked at his brother in confusion…shook his head

"Probably still sleeping as well, didn't check time correctly" he thought walking out of the bathroom to his own room. He laid down on the bed and quickly checked his phone, he put it away and immediately checked it again.

03:14

His brother wasn't mistaken. He really had stood there in front of the mirror for two hours and couldn't even remember it...He thought he had just dozed of a little after the rehearsal and not to make a fool of himself he tried to play it of as a joke but he now that he thought about it he couldn't really remember what happened there too.

He shook his head.

"Just calm down Dan...there must be a rational reason for this..." he said to himself. He stood up and went back to the bathroom. He didn't look in the mirror but just took some water.

As if something was calling to him he felt the need to look up.

"Mirror, mirror on the wall..." he whispered.

"Hello Danny, I have been waiting for you," a deep voice replied. A face appeared in the mirror.

"What the..."

"Come Danny, I have been waiting for you," the voice repeated. Danny stretched out his arm and touched the mirror and suddenly everything went dark.

Chapter 3:

Daphne opened the door of the gym to find it empty. Mrs Brown probably was somewhere else in the building and it was far before 4 o 'clock but she just couldn't wait anymore sitting at home doing nothing. She had called Danny but he didn't pick up, so she went to school, if anything she could practice her lines in front of the mirror. She put her bag on a chair and walked towards the stage. Mrs Brown had been busy, yesterday the gym was empty except from some chairs and the stage. Now, the whole gym was filled with chairs. Daphne imagined the whole gym being full and her on stage.

"Mirror…mirror…on the wall," she said.

"Daphne!!"

She stood still. Did she hear her name?

"Hello?" she said uncertain. No reply. She shrugged and walked on the stage. The mirror was hanging on the wall. She checked behind it to see if Mrs Brown left her laptop there but sadly she hadn't done that.

"Well, I guess I will have to pretend the mirror is speaking back," she said.

"Slave in the magic mirror, come from the farthest space, through wind and darkness I summon thee. Speak! Let me see thy face," she chanted in a dramatic way. She looked at the mirror. In a lower voice she said:

"What wouldst thou know, my queen?"

"Mirror, mirror on the wall, who is the fairest one of all?" she continued in her own voice. The mirror started to change. To her shock a face appeared. It was Danny.

"Daphne! Get out of here! There is something here…it lured me in…it wants to get you, get out of here!"

Daphne looked in bewilderment. "Danny…" she reached out with her arm

"Noooooooooooooooooooo!" he shouted. She touched the glass of the mirror and suddenly everything went dark

She opened her eyes and found herself in an area surrounded by mirrors all looking back at her.

"Danny?" she said looking around. Her reflections did the same except for one.

She looked at it. It looked straight back at her, its eyes started
to gleam red.
"Hello there Daphne, I have been waiting for you,"
Daphne walked backwards looking away from the red glowing
eyes into another reflection, whose eyes also started to gleam.
"Oh no, Daphne, you can't escape from me. I am everywhere,
" it said in her voice.
"Boo" she heard from behind her she turned and fell on the
ground.
"What do you want from me?!" she shouted. "Where is
Danny?!"
"Danny is not important right now nor will he ever be again
and what do I want from you?" the mirror image smiled. "Your
body, my kind sweet Daphne,"
Daphne looked at the reflection. "My...my body?"
"Yes...you and your boyfriend are the way for me and my
brother to escape this mirror world!" the reflection said
grinning.
"Danny is not my..."
"Keep telling yourself that child, we have been stuck here for
since the sixties, only ever been able to look out and never
being able to go back again,"
"Since the...wait...the frame of the mirror was from the
sixties...you performed Snowwhite and got trapped in the
mirror?" Daphne said.
"Yes, I played the Queen, my brother the huntsman and due to
some stupid bad luck we got stuck here like you are now. But
now we can finally go back to live a full life as you and Danny,"
"Nooo...nooo...I won't allow it!"
"How are you going to stop me child? You think you are here?
No...your body is still standing in front of the mirror watching
its own reflection. I just need to get back there faster than you

and I will control your body and you will be stuck...for
eternity!"
The mirror image suddenly stepped out of the frame.
"And I know which mirror I need to go to, you don't," she
taunted and ran away. Daphne stood up and ran after her but
quickly lost her between all the mirrors. She turned left and
saw a smile. Her best friend ran around the corner.
"Daphne!"
"Dan!" she said and quickly gave him a hug.
"We need to get out of here before our mirror images take
over our bodies," she said.
Dan nodded "Yeah...mine also gave me the speech...we need
to hurry, I need to get back to my bathroom mirror.
"We need to stop them first..." Daphne said thinking hard.
"How?" Danny asked raising his eyebrows?"
"I got something in my head, we need to find them first and
then I'll inform you. Let's split up," she said.
They split up and Daphne ran towards what looked like an
intersection between mirrors when she suddenly saw her
mirror image.
"Well well...you caught up with me...what now?" the mirror
image gloated. At that same moment Two Dans also appeared.
One Dan gave her a smile and she nodded. Very quickly she
took a mirror of the wall and held it front of her.
"What are you trying to do? Make me reflect on my life's
decisions?" The mirror image turned around to see that Dan
put another mirror there. She turned around and Daphne had
put another mirror around the reflections of Danny and
Daphne. This continued until they were completely
surrounded.
"Ever heard of the Droste effect?" Daphne gloated now?
"Looks like you two are stuck there...for eternity," She and

Danny high fived each other and quickly made their ways to their mirrors which were pretty close to each other.
"Okay, see you on the other side Daphne, I'll have to hurry to get to school in time for the play," Danny joked. Daphne laughed and stepped through her mirror.

Chapter 4:

She felt like she had just woken up when she suddenly realized she was staring in the mirror. She quickly looked away but it looked like the magic spell or whatever it was in the frame was broken. She checked her watch. Just 4 pm. She smiled and checked her phone. A message from Danny: On my way
She got dressed in her Evil Queen outfit and Mrs Brown had asked two of her friends to do the make-up. At 8 pm the show started. The beautiful queen wished for a daughter with a skin as white as snow, hair as black as ebony and lips as red as blood. Then she died after giving birth and the good king married a new queen.
She walked up on stage:
"Slave in the magic mirror, come from the farthest space, through wind and darkness I summon thee. Speak! Let me see thy face," she chanted in a dramatic way. She looked at the mirror and recorded Rory's face appeared on the mirror.
"What wouldst thou know, my queen?"
"Mirror, mirror on the wall, who is the fairest one of all?"
The play continued and from back stage she watched as Danny was doing his part as the huntsman. There was something weird about him but she couldn't figure out what...then she realized and she screamed. He was holding his crossbow in his left hand.
Danny was right handed.

Short Story 2 # Carpe Diem

For whoever reads this

Today was the day I would change everything.

I had a terrible fight with my fiance last night, I resorted to
drinking and that's the last thing I remember. I have a terrible
headache.
But in the middle of all this I had a revelation. I need to do
things differently, no more drinking, no more smoking, taking
care of my shit and make sure that I will never ever let this
beautiful woman go. She is my life, she is my everything and
till yesterday I didn't realize this and I almost lost her.
She was gone in the morning when I woke up. I hope I am not
too late. I sent her a message but no reply yet.
I'm late, I have to go to my job. As shitty as it might be, it is still
my job. Even though the headache is killing me I can't take a
sick day. I need the money and in order to get my life in order I
need to go work. I quickly got dressed and went out. It was
only a short walk to work. At work, as usual my colleagues
mostly ignored me. It was copy writing, sitting in a cubicle at a
desk working on documents all fucking day long. It was boring
work but at least it paid the bills.
It was strange, normally I would get work related phone calls
during the day but today was quiet. I checked my own phone
and saw that she hadn't replied yet. That is weird...normally
she would. I sent her another message.
Around lunch time I stayed at my desk, I didn't feel hungry at
home, still didn't feel hungry. The headache was still there.
What on earth did I drink last night?
Colleagues sometimes came across my cubicle and stared.

Almost sad or disgusted...I checked to make sure I didn't come to work without pants but there they were and clean ones too. I checked my phone again. She replied: Stop texting me!

My heart broke. I felt my breathing getting heavy. No no no... what did I say...what did I do? Whatever it is we can talk about this? Can't we...

I sent a message back.

It was difficult to concentrate but I tried. I tried to focus on my work, I opened another boring document. I was suddenly reminded of this old game I used to play: Phantasmagoria: A puzzle of Flesh. Where the lead character, also wearing a gray shirt like me coincidentally was doing the same kind of boring job in a cubicle. His computer was haunted and insulting him. Mine, luckily...or unluckily was a boring piece of shit. My phone buzzed.

She replied: I don't know who you are but this isn't funny, stop texting me!

Who I am...what the hell was that supposed to mean? Sure, we had a big fight but we had fights before, this wasn't a reason to suddenly pretend I do not exist. I threw my phone on my desk and tried to forget about it. I would go see her tonight and we'll talk about this and everything will be good.

Today was the day I would change everything.

How I wished that like the main character in Phantasmagoria I had a gay best friend colleague being able to cheer me up right now. We could go get some ice cream or something. But no... like always everyone around me was ignoring me, only focused on themselves. They didn't even greet me...or each other in the morning. Come to think of it, I don't think I have seen my supervisor for over three weeks now.

At 3 pm I checked my cellphone. No messages or calls or anything. I texted my fiance telling her I wanted to talk to her and would see her tonight.
My headache, if anything seemed to be getting worse. I should have taken some painkillers with me but I forgot. I didn't feel any hunger or thirst. I just wanted to get this job over with and go see her. I would buy her flowers and tell her I was sorry and we would make things right and that I was going to change my act. I was going to be the man that she deserved.
Today was the day I would change everything.
At 5 pm I was finally allowed to leave this boring as hell job and I walked out as soon as I could. The person walking in front of me closed the door as if I wasn't there but then again...that kind of rudeness I would expect from some people. I checked my phone as I walked out with another colleague and saw that she read my message but didn't reply. What on earth did I do yesterday...why can't I remember? And why won't this headache go away. All questions for later. I needed to go to the mall to buy the biggest bouquet of flowers she had ever seen.
Luckily it wasn't far to the mall, in hindsight it might have been quicker if I had gone with the car this morning but I think she took it as I don't remember seeing it in the garage. Then again...remembering things seems to be difficult.
I need to focus I told myself. I arrived at the mall to discover it was closed.
Dammit...closed today? Of all days! Resigned I sat on the ground against the wall. Today was not my day. But I decided there and then that I'm not going to let that little thing destroy my promise.
Today was the day I would change everything.
I stood back up and went to the park and checked if anybody

was watching me. Nobody was. I carefully picked one of the most beautiful roses I had ever seen. Just in time too, the sky was getting dark and it started raining. I quickly ran out of the park and towards her home, an apartment not that far from where I live.

I was soaking wet when I arrived there and of course I didn't have the keys with me so I called her apartment number.

"Hello?" her voice, her beautiful voice sounded over the speaker, it was like the best thing I ever wanted to hear.

"It's me," I said happily. She hung up. For a second I was dumbfounded. No, she wouldn't. I rang again.

"Go away!" she shouted.

"Honey! Don't hang up! I know we had a fight and I said some terrible things but please let's talk about this, I love you! I love you to the end of the world...I wanted to buy a big bouquet of flowers for you but the mall was closed so I picked this beautiful rose for you. I am so sorry for everything I said. I am going to change honey! Today is the day I will change everything! Honey...please let me in...I'm so cold...and so wet... please let me in honey...please..." I shouted, I cried, I begged her to let me in. I heard her cry to and then she hung up.

I dropped the rose in front of the building and turned around. In the rain and cold wind I walked towards home. I cried...it was so unfair! She couldn't do this to me! Could she? No...it was my fault and my fault alone. I was too late...I didn't change when I should have...but would it have been too late? I can't believe that. I mustn't believe that.

Today was the day I would change everything

I walked towards my front door. It was open. Did I leave it open? I couldn't remember. It's a good thing this

neighborhood is pretty safe. Inside, everything was as it was
supposed to be. I guess I should make some dinner but I
wasn't hungry…I wasn't feeling anything. Except for this damn
headache.
I turned on the television. The local news…always very
interesting stuff of course I said sarcastically.
Apparently the mayor gave a big speech for his re-election,
some new roads were going to be build and I am just as bored
as you are right now.
"And finally, last night a drunk driver drove himself of the
bridge and into the river…the police and fire brigade were able
to pull the car out of the water but they were too late to save
the driver who was identified as a local man…"
I watched the footage of the car being dragged out and my
eyes widened and suddenly everything became clear. People
ignoring me, my fiance asking who I was, asking me to stop
texting her. Her crying at her apartment building. In that one
single moment, everything became crystal clear

Today was the day that I died

Short story 3 # Dinner for seven

A man in a tailored suit was running around the mansion in great haste. His task complete he needed to perform one final step and get out of there. He entered the study and closed the door.
"Here…it should be somewhere here…" he mumbled to himself. He opened the drawer of the big oak desk on the opposite side of the room to find an envelope there. The man smiled despite himself. He opened it and in it was a note, a big amount of money, more money than he had ever seen and a small pill.

Dear Maxwell,
Great job, with this money you can get out of here and start a new life if necessary, or you can take the other option…
I'm sorry old boy, I wish there was another way…
R.
PS. Please destroy this note after reading it

Maxwell pocketed the money and the pill and threw the note into the fireplace, then he walked outside the study through the hallway and the mansion. He got inside his piece of trash called a car and drove off.
"Tssss…other option indeed…" he said to himself. The farther he got away from the house the more happy he felt. He was free, he was rich. Suddenly he thought he saw something of the road and then his tire exploded. The car rolled over against a tree and newly rich Maxwell was dead.
From a car a bit further away a man stepped out and walked over.
"I'm sorry old boy, I wish there was another way," he said

looking at the dead body in the car. The man reached inside the pockets of Maxwell and got the pill and the money.
The man sat down against the tree and got a cigarette from out of a fancy box from his pocket. He lighted it.
"I really do…I really do…but I had to do this you know. There were just too many wrongs here and people need to learn to pay the price. That includes everyone…you and me and so the others…"

The table was decorated. The food was ready and Maxwell and his colleague Yvette were waiting at the door when the first guest arrived. The doorbell rang and Maxwell opened. A beautiful young woman stepped inside. Brown long hair, green eyes.
"Miss Eva Ives, I presume, may I take your coat?" Maxwell asked bowing slightly.
"You may…mister…" Miss Ives said smiling softly.
"Just Maxwell, Miss Ives, this is Yvette, we will be your servants for the evening," Maxwell said taking her coat and hanging it near the door.
"Thank you Maxwell," Miss Ives said. She walked with Yvette to the dining room. The doorbell rang another time.
An older bulky man with pleasant eyes and a dark gray suit stood in front of the door.
"Hello there! I got an invitation to come here," he said holding a letter in his hand.
"Yes, yes, I know all about it. Mister Adam McDuffy right?" Maxwell said.
"Indeed good sir, and you might be?"
"Maxwell sir, just Maxwell, me and my colleague Yvette will be your servants this evening," Max well said quickly. Mister McDuffy walked inside and Maxwell took his coat.

"Strange thing, a letter...you would think nowadays people would sent an e-mail," he said.

"Well, our employer is sometimes old fashioned...but please sir, don't let him know I said that," Maxwell said.

McDuffy laughed. "No worries, good man," Maxwell guided the rotund man to the dining room when the doorbell rang another time.

"Yvette, I'll let you handle introductions. I go open the door," he said hurriedly pacing back to the door

One by one the guests of the evening came in. Mr Richard Brown, Mrs Lena Cox, Miss Robin Rhodes, Mr Maximilian Graves, Mr Rory Smith.

They all settled in the dining room. After all the introductions were done. Miss Rhodes asked the question that was on everyone's minds.

"Why are we here Maxwell?" she asked in a sharp voice, not entirely friendly.

"To have dinner, Miss," Maxwell simply replied.

"So you are telling me that your employer send out dinner invitations and doesn't show up himself?" McDuffy said.

"What is this? "And then there were none"?" the big man said laughing at his own joke.

"Of course not sir, we're not on an island," Maxwell said matter-of-factly. "Please, sirs, madams, I have my instructions, please allow me to carry them out for you," He nodded to Yvette. Yvette went to the kitchen and came back with plates full of a delicious smelling soup.

Maxwell filled the wine glasses.

"Enjoy, sirs, madams, if there is anything you require just ring the bell, me and Yvette at your service,"

The seven guests slowly eat their soup.

"Well...if no one is going to talk I will start, this is a rather awkward situation but not unlike we have seen before right or not Rory?" Mr Brown said.

Mr Rory Smith laughed. "True...I remember this one night in Vegas,"

"Oh please, spare us these tales of young men doing wild things in Vegas," Mrs Cox said. "As if Vegas was only created 10 years ago," she said and winked to Mr Graves and McDuffy. They both grinned sheepishly back.

"Well, personally I never been to Vegas, if I would go to the USA I rather go to Yellowstone or the Grand Canyon," Miss Ives said.

"That's sooo boring," Mr Smith said. "You should live a little,"

"You don't know me Mr Smith, maybe I have already," she said. Then laughed.

"So, does anyone have any idea why we are here?" Mr Graves asked.

"To have dinner apparently but that can't be all of it...where is our host?" McDuffy answered.

"I guess we will have to look for the common denominator between us," Miss Rhodes guessed.

"So...what we have in common that the host would have invited all of us here...hmmm, well Mr Smith and I have been friends for a while, I am acquainted with Graves and McDuffy," Brown said.

"And I have known Graves and McDuffy for years now too," Mrs Cox said. "Anyone else?" Everybody but Miss Ives nodded.

"So everybody but Miss Ives knows Mr Graves and McDuffy," Mr Smith said. "What does that mean? Does anyone know Miss Ives?"

Everybody shook their heads.

"So it looks I am the odd one out?" Miss Ives said. "I don't know any of you and you seem to know at least Graves and

McDuffy, what is the connection?"
Maxwell and Yvette came back into the room with the main course.
"Maxwell, will our host be joining us later?" McDuffy asked.
"Not that I know of sir, it's not in my instructions," Maxwell replied. They both left. An awkward silence fell.
"So, guessing from your clothes and trips to Vegas I can guess you all have quite a bit of money," Miss Ives said none judgmentally.
"As do you Miss Ives,"
"Correct," she replied smiling. "So, like our host we are all wealthy," she concluded.
"Well…if you want to put it that way," Mr Smith said.
"I don't feel like mincing words Mr Smith, I am not ashamed of being rich, neither should you," she replied. They started eating. McDuffy stood up after eating and lighted a cigarette from a fancy cigarette box.
"Are you okay?" Mrs Cox asked.
"Yes, yes, but sometimes I just prefer standing a bit, especially after a meal," he said.
Maxwell and Yvette came in once more with desert. They ate it all and Maxwell guided them to the living room where they all set down. Yvette started pouring drinks.
"I believe it's time to read you the letter our employee gave me," Maxwell said. Unfolding a letter from his pocket.

"All,
I have to say that at one point I envied you all. You are rich,
have acquired a certain amount of fame and you live a life
many would be envious off. I was envious, until I got rich
myself and could do all the things you do.
Having said that, I have come to the realization that being rich

Maxwell looked up. All seven guests were sprawled on their seats...dead. Yvette, who had been snooping of the dishes in the kitchen was laying on the floor as well.
Maxwell closed the letter and threw it in the fire and he ran outside the room towards the study...
In the living room Mister **R**ory Smith opened his eyes. He looked around and smiled. He quickly went over to McDuffy and took out of his pocket his fancy cigarette box. He then quickly went out after Maxwell...

Rory looked at Maxwell one last time.
"I truly am sorry...but nobody can know," he said. He stood up and walked to his car. He sat down closed the door and put the key in the ignition. He suddenly realized he wasn't alone.
"Miss Ives...how did you?"
"Really "Mr Smith" Do you think we rich people are all that stupid?" she said annoyed pointing a gun at his head.
"But I saw you eat..." Rory said.
"Yes...but I don't eat a lot so the poison didn't affect me as much, now...take that pill you got back from Maxwell, I rather

not shoot you and leave evidence," she said.
"Come now Miss Ives, you really think I would not have prepared for this?" he said. "I told you, everyone, including me has to pay the price.
He turned the ignition and the car exploded.

Short story 4 # Beth

"Fuck you Murphy! And fuck your mother too!"
"I'm sorry, could you repeat that?" The ship's pleasant female artificial intelligence's voice came from the speaker.
"Eh…never mind…just Murphy 's Law…I just need to lose contact with you and then it'll be complete," Commander Malcolm Rush said shaking his head.
There was no response.
"Please tell me you're just fucking with me now,"
"Yes, sorry…couldn't resist," the computer said. Malcolm made a crude gesture to the speaker.
"Your silence indicates you just flipped me the bird, might I remind you that this is very much out of protocol, Commander," the computer said.
"This whole mission is out of protocol at the moment," Malcolm grunted. He knelt down at his controller port and flipped open a panel.
"I will need to get my steering back first, how about you give me some advice," he said.
"Of course commander, I will try and get contact with mission control in the meantime," the computer answered. It guided Malcolm to the steps of getting his steering back and it worked.
Malcolm stood up.
"Good, steering is back…now I will need thrust, any news yet on communications?"
"Sadly nothing yet, Commander,"
Malcolm again shook his head. He gathered his tools and looked outside of his cockpit towards the star that seemed to be getting closer. In reality of course he was getting closer to the star, caught in its gravity. Thinking of this he quickly

snapped back to reality and walked towards the back of the ship where the engines were. Luckily for him it was not a particularly big ship.

"Computer, you are still there?" he asked.

"Ready and waiting your command, Commander," the computer said.

"Please call me Malcolm, if I'm going to die at least it would be nice if someone called my name," he said sitting down opening a shaft that led to engine. He crawled inside.

"If you insist, Malcolm," the computer said.

"Do you have a name?" Malcolm asked knowing the answer.

"I am just an AI, we don't have names,"

"Would you like one?" Malcolm asked crawling a bit further. "I should not have eaten a burger for breakfast," he mumbled to himself.

"I never really considered it," the computer said.

"I think you should have one, any ideas?" Malcolm said turning around on his back and looking straight into the engine.

"Nobody has ever asked me for my opinion before, it's kind of unusual," the computer said.

"Might be, but I'm asking you now, I'm not going out calling my computer, computer so you better think of something. There must be something that you like, you do after all have a sense of humor," he said while using a tool to loosen some bolts on another panel. "Panels, panels, panels...they really enjoy panels on star ships don't they..."

"Well, sure...they installed every pop culture material of the last few centuries in my database, I can pick a name from that," the computer said.

"You do that, meanwhile I have to unscrew at least four more panels before I can even start with the thruster, do we still have time?"

"Not much, but yes, we still have time," the computer said. Malcolm nodded realizing that the computer could not see that. He unscrewed the panels and immediately saw what was wrong. Luckily he had the replacements part aboard. Unluckily he had to crawl out of the shaft and go get it. He went back and stood up.

"If I am going to survive this I really am going to shuffle stuff around here," he said. He walked to a storage compartment on the opposite of where he was now and got the part that needed to be replaced. He crawled back in.

"Beth," the computer said.

"Beth?" Malcolm asked.

"That's my name, Beth,"

"Okay," Malcolm nodded approvingly. "Nice to meet you Beth, I am Malcolm,"

"Yes, I knew that already," Beth answered. Malcolm was back at the engine now. He removed the old part and installed the new part. Closed all the panels again and crawled back out.

"Beth, can you test this engine now,"

"Engine is running at 30% capacity, this won't be enough to escape the gravity,"

"I figured, I'm going to check the other engine as well," Malcolm said. Walking back into storage to get another spare part just in case. He opened another panel and started the back breaking crawl again.

"I have some good news Malcolm, I have reestablished contact with mission control,"

"Great news! Patch them through," Malcolm said, smiling for the first time.

"Commander Rush, this is mission control, what is your situation?" a male said on the intercom.

"This is Commander Rush, situation is bad, I am caught in the gravity of a star and plunging towards it, one engine is running on 30 % capacity and I'm checking to see if I can fix the other, oh and my computer named herself Beth,"
It was silent on the comm and then they replied:
"Eh...noted. We will sent...Beth some additional data that may help you in getting more power out of your engines,"
"Thanks mission control,"
"Data received. I have sent it to your datapad, Commander," Beth said. Malcolm reached in his pocket and nodded.
"Excellent, just what I needed," he said. He had arrived at the second engines, removed the panels and got to work.
"Beth, sent over my data to Mission Control, then at least I have partially completed my mission," Malcolm said. He closed the panels and crawled out of the the narrow space.
"We have received your data commander, this is very valuable information," Mission control said.
"I thought so, Beth, run a check on the engines,"
"Engines are now operating on a 55 % capacity," Beth answered.
"It will have to do," Malcolm said. He made his way back to the cock pit and sat down.
"Well, here goes nothing," he said and flipped the switch to start the engine.
Nothing happened.
He did it again.
Nothing happened.
"Third times a charm!" he said and flipped the switch. A low buzzing from behind him made him sink in his seat as if it were the sweetest sound he ever heard.
"Nicely done Beth, Mission control," he sighed out of relief. He turned the ship around to finally not look into the star

anymore but just the cold blackness of space. He checked his readings and noticed that while he had slowed down his movement towards the star he was still going.

"Mission control, I still am not having the required speed to reach escape velocity, any ideas?" he said a lot more calmly than he felt.

"We are discussing this now, standby," Mission control said.

"There is not much else I can do..." Malcolm said. "Beth, anything in your enormous brain that can help?"

"I am looking now Malcolm," Beth said.

"Commander, we want you to jettison everything that is not required to fly the ship. Escape pod, cargo, personal items,"

"Acknowledged, mission control," Malcolm said. Getting up and walking aft. He quickly gathered everything that could be jettisoned, it wasn't much and put it in the escape pod. He didn't mind losing it as he would have no use for it on this place. The escape pod would bring him even faster to his death then this ship would. He walked back into the cockpit and activated the pod from his control panel.

"Why would they have that button here..." he wondered out loud.

"Normally a captain would go down with his ship, this allows the captain to safely jettison his crew with the escape pod without exposing himself to vacuum," Beth answered.

"Right...." Malcolm said. He saw a sudden increase in his speed and he finally started to move slowly away from the star.

"That did it mission control! We are on our way out!" he said.

"Good news Commander, we are eager to debrief..." Suddenly and out of nowhere a big asteroid that was also pulled in by the gravity of the star hit the ship and it turned around knocking out one of the engines. Malcolm who had not fastened his seat belt was flung across the cock pit into a panel.

"Of course…" he said with great pain "It had to be a panel…"

"Commander Rush, what happened?" Mission control asked.

"Asteroid…hit…flung across cockpit…" he said. He felt his chest…bruised or broken ribs…fun times.

"Malcolm…one of the engines is knocked out…we are getting drawn back into the star," Beth said.

"Give me a second," Malcolm said breathing hard. He slowly walked back to his seat and got out the medkit from the side of his chair. He quickly took some painkillers.

"Your AI is right, one of the engines is knocked out," mission control said.

"Okay, noted, I'm going back there," Malcolm said getting up. The painkillers luckily worked quickly. He made his way back to the engines and started his crawl back. It was even more difficult this time.

"Malcolm…is it okay if I am afraid," Beth asked. Malcolm pondered that question for a second.

"Yes Beth, it is okay to be afraid if you are about to die, computer or not," he said in a calm voice.

"Thank you…because I am afraid,"

"Me too, Beth…me too," Malcolm said removing another panel.

He looked at the engine and got his datapad.

"I am open for any suggestions," he said to Beth and mission control. He made a scan of the engine and sent it too mission control. They quickly replied back with a plan to get the engine fixed enough. As quickly as he could he fixed it. Put the panels back and crawled out. Out of breath he asked:

"Beth, test please,"

"I'm sorry Malcolm…engine power is at 45%, it won't be enough,"

"That's okay Beth…at least I have you here," Malcolm said. He sat down against the wall.
"If it is any comfort, I'm glad that you are here as well Malcolm," Beth said. Malcolm smiled.
"Goodbye mission control, thanks for trying,"

Short story #5 – Safe harbor

Nathan looked outside the broken window, zombies were at the door trying to break in. He had gotten used to the sounds and he knew he was relatively safe for the moment but he had to get out of there and back to Harbor. People were counting on him to do so. He pulled his backpack towards him and looked inside.
"Flashlight, bandages, water…yes, definitely worth the effort," he said to himself. He slung the backpack across his shoulders. He pulled his gun out of its holster on his left leg and checked the ammo.
"Hmmm, less good news here…only four bullets…"
He put the gun back in his holster and checked that his combat knife was in place. It was. He wasn't really planning on using it. Best strategy was always to run. He was a runner. He had always run, even before the incident. Back then it was a hobby, a sport. Now it was his way to survive. The fact that he could run was the reason why people at Harbor allowed him in. Nathan could see why in the future people might find it unbelievable that you won't help someone unless they are able to help you but he didn't find anything wrong with it. Not when there are zombies knocking on your door trying to eat you. He had some experience with the gun now but he preferred not using it. It was loud and would only attract more zombies and unlike the silencers on TV, they weren't really making the noise that much more silent. Oh tv…
"Damn…I'm sure I miss Netflix now…" he mumbled to himself. He tightened the straps from his backpack. The water was pretty heavy. He had to look for an exit or a way to get down. The front door was no option. He decided to go up to the roof. He climbed two stairs and then got to the roof exit of the small

convenient store...well, what was left of the convenient store. He pulled his gun and knife and slowly opened the door. With his gun in his left hand and the knife in his right he looked around, listening for the slow gurgling sound. At 10 meters away he saw the remains of a body. A bit further there was indeed a zombie. The zombie turned slowly around he had a shirt on with the logo of the store in bright red on it.

"I guess you were the owner," Nathan said. "I'm so sorry..." He ran up to him and stabbed the zombified store owner in the head killing it. He quickly looked around, no more zombies here. He quickly closed the door of the roof exit and looked around. The emergency stairs were on the side of the building. If he was lucky the zombies would not have thought of coming there.

"Heh...thought..." Nathan chuckled. It's not like zombies actually could think, although they did have a tendency to go for doors so there must be something that constitutes instinct or so. If there were still scientists around what would they say? Nathan did his best Neil Degrasse Tyson impression: "What are you asking me for, I'm your personal astrophysicist, go ask Richard Dawkins,"

"Well, I'm a biologist, not a virologist...if this even is a caused by a virus that is," he continued in his mock British accent. Yes, they would first argue about who was allowed to answer the question, come to think of it...he didn't know any famous virologists. Nathan walked towards the emergency stairs and looked down. No zombies there. He slowly climbed down being careful not to make any noise. It was scary...the stairs were not well maintained and risking any sound would cause for this way to be blocked. Nathan was hardly able to breath. When he finally was down he took a moment to collect himself. Then he walked away from the building in a hurried but silent pace.

After 100 meters he started to relax a bit. The building was out of sight now and blocked by the trees. For now he was safe. Unless zombies strolled around in the forest. Which could always be the case. He walked towards the forest. It was getting dark now.

"One of these days I should try and find a watch..." he said to himself. He totally had forgotten to watch the sun. In the dark it was more difficult to navigate and avoid zombies. Luckily, these zombies didn't become more active at night like in most fiction he read or watched. He heard gurgling sounds coming in front of him. He looked around and saw a big tree to the left of him, he walked in a crouch towards it and hid behind it. He heard the gurgling sound coming closer. There were at least three of them. The gurgling sound was now right next to him and then it moved further away. Nathan still hold his breath for another 20 seconds then he breathed deeply and left his hiding spot.

He looked around and saw the mark he left there earlier this day to indicate he was still going to the right way. The forest was now completely dark. Slowly and carefully Nathan walked towards the road to Harbor.

Harbor was of course not the original name of the small town that was converted into a anti zombie fortress but everybody called it that. It was a small community of farmers, former military (seeing as there was no real government anymore) and runners like Nathan. The military protected the farmers and the runners ran around the area to collect things that could not be farmed by farmers. Runners were highly respected because they took many risks and many never made it back. Nathan had collected at least three runner bags in the past and had to kill some of his former colleagues when he encountered them in zombie form. They also had to go further and further away. Now his daily tracks sometimes brought him 10 km away from Harbor, about an hour worth of running.

"And I used to do this for fun…" he mumbled to himself.

Nathan finally cleared the forest and came to the road. He looked both ways. "Left, right, left, so you know there are no zombies trying to run you over,"

He saw a car wreckage on the road. It was completely picked clean by other scavengers, maybe even some of his own people. He knew that he had to go the other way to Harbor. He did a small warm up and started doing what his job title said he would. He ran. At a moderate pace. No need to exhaust yourself if you were not being chased. But he did want to get home fast, not only where the guards always very cranky at night. He also didn't like staying out in the open. Zombies were not his only enemies.

You would expect that when the whole world went to hell people would unit all under one banner. But no…humanity is shitty like that, some people are only looking out for themselves and a single runner with a full bag is quite a tasty target for those deplorable raiders. He also had to watch out for random crap laying on the road. Car parts, corpses, both human and zombie and other random crap that he had no real understanding on how they came to be there. Nathan suddenly stopped. In front of him there were a whole horde of zombies just standing, minding their own business. They hadn't noticed him. He quickly but silently went off the road. There was no forest here only a road verge that was inclined. He climbed down and made his way past the horde. For at least 25 meters more he walked there, then made his way up. He looked at the horde, they still hadn't noticed him. He turned around and then tripped on a wheel case, making what would seem the loudest noise ever. The horde turned into his direction as one and started moving towards him.

"Oh shit!" he yelled. He stood up, kicked the wheel case aside and started to run. He tried to remember his breathing techniques. The zombies were now chasing him and while he was faster than them there growling would attract more attention and he still had to watch where he was going. As predicted other zombies came from the side of the roads as well.

"Ooooh….the guards are going to be pissed…' Nathan thought. He tried to think of something suddenly remembering he had a flashlight with him. While running he got it out of his bag and flipped it on. Somehow zombies were very attracted to light and here in the total dark it might help him to get rid of at least some of them.

He stopped and shined the light into the zombies' faces and then threw it to the side of the road. A large group of them went after it. Nathan smiled and turned around looking a zombie right in the face. He quickly got his knife and stabbed it in the head. He heard more gurgling and started to run for his life. After another two kilometers on the road he finally saw the gates of Harbor showing up. The zombie horde was still walking after him but he had a big lead. He ran towards the gate.

"Zombie horde….coming…" he said breathing hard

"Hi to you too Nathan," the guard said jokingly.

"Yeah…yeah…we'll talk later…I like to get in," Nathan said.

"Of course," the guard said. He nodded down and another guard opened the small gate.

"Next time, try not to bring uninvited guests," the guard said.

"I'll make it up to you, I got some comic books from my last haul, want one?" Nathan said. The guard smiled.

"Sure! Now, let's get rid of these guests of yours and we'll talk," the guard said. He and Nathan walked up the barricade where the other guards already were ready with their guns. Nathan smiled as the zombies fell. He was home. He was in safe Harbor.

Short story 6 – The Writing Zone

"Come on...you can do it," David said to himself.
"Don't just stare at the blank screen, just fucking type," he said
a bit louder. He pushed his laptop away and stood up. This
wasn't helping. He had sworn he would be able to finish this
book. His publisher was waiting on it. He booked a hotel in a
small town somewhere far removed from everything and
everyone to finish it. He decided he needed some fresh air. He
had been sitting in this room for almost eight hours now with
nothing to show for it.
He opened his hotel door and walked down towards the lobby.
"Ah, Mister Banks, good morning to you," the receptionist said.
"Good morning?" he checked his watch...it was indeed
morning. Apparently he had been awake all night but he was
sure that it was day last time he checked. So...not 8
hours....but longer.
"Yes, isn't it a lovely day, any plans?" the receptionist asked.
David looked at the man and forced a smile. There were
already enough rumors of him being an anti-social, autistic
shut in as there were. And he was not a shut in!
"I'm going for a walk, I would like to have breakfast when I'm
back," he said. The receptionist nodded.
"Of course, sir, enjoy your walk, the hills are especially lovely in
the morning,"
"I'll go there then, see you later," David said leaving the hotel.
It was a lovely spring morning although David was happy be
was wearing his jacket. He made his way to the hills and
started to walk across a narrow path surrounded by trees. He
was enjoying himself whistling a little tune and taking big gulps
of air. He felt inspired, story ideas were floating in his head.
He closed his eyes when he suddenly tripped and fell down.

"Of course…" he mumbled looking backwards expecting a
root. Instead he saw a shoe with a foot and leg attached with a
whole body attached. A dead body. The man had two big
slashes in his chest and his dead eyes stared directly at David.
David turned around and made his way back to the hotel.
"Police…dead…body…quick…phone…" he said to the
receptionist out of breath. The receptionist stood up and
immediately dialed the alarm number. David told the person
on the line what he had discovered. Not an hour later the
police had picked him up and he guided them to the dead
body. The victim was like David a tourist staying in the hotel.
He gave a statement and was brought back to the hotel with
instructions not to leave the area. David barely ate that day, he
sat in his room thinking about what he had discovered and
stared at the empty screen of his word processor. He typed:
"Murder in the hill"
Well, for a temporary title it was pretty good. He realized how
stupid it might be to write about an active murder
investigation, people might think he'd done it. Still, it was the
only thing he could think about so he started to write. When
David finally was able to write he ended up in some sort of
"zone" as he would like to call it. He would lose track of
everything around him furiously typing and deleting stuff.
After a while he snapped out of it. He looked at his document
and was pretty happy with the result. He saved it and went
outside. It should be around dinner time now he thought. He
went down in the lobby.
"Good morning Mister Banks, how are you today?" The
receptionist said smiling.
"Good morning?" he checked his watch…it was indeed
morning. He hadn't realized he was so much in the zone.
"Eh..good morning," he said. "I am going out for a walk…been

writing a long time, need some fresh air, preferably without dead bodies," he said.

"Yes, I understand, sir. Why don't you try to be beach, it will be lovely there today," the receptionist said. David nodded and left the hotel.

He walked towards the beach and felt the wind ruffle his hair. He felt for the first time a bit more relaxed then yesterday. I guess he got lucky that he had a bit of fame otherwise the police might have been more on his case. He was on the beach now which seemed completely empty. The water was of course too cold to swim so only people who wanted to walk their dog would go there. At the moment...nobody did. He walked across the shore line when he suddenly saw something big laying on the ground. He walked closer and it was another dead body. Again with two big slashes across his chest. The dead eyes were staring at him. He ran back to the Hotel.

"Should have taken my cellphone!" he cursed himself walking in the hotel.

"Police...dead...body...quick...phone..." he said to the receptionist out of breath.

The receptionist dialed the alarm number again and David told what he had seen. The police arrived quickly and took him to the body.

"Where were you last night?" the officer asked.

"I was in my room, writing" David said.

"Can you prove that?" the officer asked.

"Well, there is a time stamp on when I saved last, this morning but also the hotel staff should be able to tell you if I left the hotel last night," David said defensively. They made their way back to the hotel. The receptionist indeed confirmed that David hadn't left his room and also didn't use the emergency doors otherwise they would have heard an alarm.

The officer nodded.

"Okay, thank you...you better tell your guests to stay inside. Two murders in such a short time..." the officer shook his head and walked out.

David looked at the receptionist.

"I'm going up, I would like some dinner in my room," he said.

"Of course sir," the receptionist said making a note on his pad.

David went to his room and sat there staring outside.

"What is going on here?" he mumbled. Half an hour later the food arrived and he ate in silence. He went back to his laptop and started writing again getting in the zone. He wrote about the second murder and how his protagonist, William Bigsby was trying to solve the murders. When he snapped out of it he noticed it was morning again.

"This is getting weird..." he said. He went down.

"Good morning Mr Banks," the receptionist said smiling.

"Good morning to you as well," he answered. "I'm going for my usual walk but I rather skip the hills or the beach," he said.

"Yes, I can imagine sir," the receptionist said. "I recommend the forest,"

David nodded and went outside towards the forest. He knew the police officer said not to leave the hotel but that was because he was afraid that another hotel guest could be murdered. From what he heard from the officers at the crime scenes the bodies were already dead for a couple of hours so he felt pretty safe. He walked into the forest and was pleasantly surprised by the smells coming from it. He walked for an hour enjoying himself and happy he didn't find any other bodies when suddenly he heard something crashing behind him.

Another dead body, this one half hanging in the tree with two big slashes and his eyes staring at him.

"Quite amazing isn't it the dead still being able to look at their murderer...if people would only notice it lots of murders could be easily solved," he heard a voice saying from behind him. He turned around. It was the receptionist.

"You have been quite busy David," he said smiling broadly. "Three murders in three days...for a newbie you are quite proficient,"

"What are you talking about?" David asked grinding his teeth.

"Oh come on, you thought I sent you to these places at random? I have been watching you David, ever since you came to us and our clan leader turned you,"

"Turned me? Turned me into what?"

"A lycan! A werewolf if you want!" the receptionist said. You didn't notice it was full moon the last couple of days?"

"No...why would I...I was in my room writing,"

"Yes you were and at 12 am you turned and each night you dragged a random guest out of the window and killed him with two slashes. I am not exactly sure why you didn't eat them but I guess that is because you were not fully fledged yet,"

"Fully fledged?"

"Yes, unless you survive the first three times you turn you won't be a full-fledged werewolf and not being able to turn at any time you want,"

"So you are saying I am fully fledged now?" David asked.

"Yes! And now we are brothers!" the receptionist said with glee. David nodded and felt an energy burning inside of him he hadn't felt before. His teeth grew, his jaw became larger, and his ears became wolf like. He bent down on all fours.

"Yes! Yes!" The receptionist said. "Embrace your new life!"

"Oh, I will," David said with a heavy growl and jumped towards the receptionist and killed him with two slashes. The dead eyes indeed stared at him.

"I will find this clan leader and kill him as well. He quickly ran out of the forest and changed back into his human form. He ran up to his room and grabbed his laptop.

"Why did you have to kill him?" a voice said behind him. He turned around and saw the police officer.

"You know dam well why, I suppose you are the so called clan leader?" David said.

"I am, my son" he said.

"I. am. Not. Your. Son!" David said. He grabbed a bottle of wine that he drank with his dinner yesterday and slammed the clan leader over the head. As the body fell on the ground David screamed a strange not human sounding scream, he had changed into a wolf again and started to eat every last bit of the clan leader. He changed back, wiped his mouth, sat down, opened his laptop and typed:

"Werewolf Hotel" – a story by David Banks.

Short story 7 – A guy, a girl and a fast food place.

I had seen her before. On a wedding I think. Beautiful long hair, eyes that seem to sparkle and a figure…wow…don't even get me started on that and now she was standing in front of me.
"Would you like fries with that?" I asked. She looked up and I think she recognized me. She smiled and said: "Yes, please," she checked my name tag. "…Daniel" I smiled back and got the fries. She walked away with her order and I followed her with my eyes. My best friend and colleague Bart poked me in the side.
"Don't let the boss catch you like this," he murmured from the side of his mouth. I focused my attention back on the new customer before me. This older lady quickly vaporized all my thoughts of this mysterious woman and I thought I would never see her again.
For the next week every time someone walked into the restaurant I got my hopes up to be completely smashed again. I stopped believing she would ever be back and kicked myself in the head (not literally of course, I am not that agile) that I didn't ask her name at least.
Then, when I didn't expect it she walked back into the restaurant. She walked up my counter. I never helped other customers as fast as I did now.
"Hello," I said.
"Hello Daniel," she said, she hadn't even looked at my name tag. I felt that my face was going red. I needed to say something.
"Soo…eh…what can I do you for, eh what can I do for you?" I said clumsily. She gave her order.
"Okay, I will have this ready in a minute, if you want I can bring

it to you," I said. She smiled and nodded and walked away. I looked at Bart who gave me a thumbs up. I prepared the food and brought it to her.

"Here you go, Miss," I said.

"You can call me Laurel if you like," she said.

"Here you go, Laurel," I said. "Say, weren't you on this wedding a couple of weeks ago?"

"I was, I thought I saw you there," she said looking me straight in my eyes. I felt myself going red again.

"I didn't think you'd notice, I mean I was sitting in the back and only there because my best friend didn't want to go alone," I said quickly.

"Yeah...I also was there so that somebody else didn't had to go alone. I actually never met de bride and groom before but it was a really nice wedding," she said.

"Yeah it was!" I said. "I'd say it's in my top three of weddings,"

"Oh? You go to weddings a lot?" she asked. I was about to answer when suddenly a stern voice behind me called my name.

"Mister Baker! You have customers waiting!"

"Yes, sir, coming right now sir," I said. I looked at her. "I'm sorry, I need to go...maybe we can continue this conversation another time,"

"Baker!" my boss yelled. I quickly went back to my register. When I looked up she was gone.

She didn't return the next day, or the day after that. Once again I felt stupid, I should have asked her number. At least I had her name now. It was the most beautiful name I ever heard...although I might be a bit biased. I dreamed about her. Remembered the whole conversation. Thinking of things I should have said and how big of an idiot I was. But she did remember me from the wedding.

"My top three of weddings...what the fuck Daniel, what were you thinking?" I said to myself.
"You never answered my question though, you know...do you go to weddings a lot?"
I looked up and looked straight in Laurel's eyes. I felt myself getting red again.
"You really ought to do something about your shyness, although it's kinda cute," she said laughing. I smiled like a little schoolboy
"So, what can I get you today?" I said.
"The usual...and maybe you can leave your phone number as well," she said.
"Yes, of course...no problem at all. It will be ready for you in a minute," I hastily said turning away. I quickly prepared her food, wrote my number on the paper place mat on the tray and brought it to her. I noticed my boss was watching me.
"Can't stay and chat, my boss is watching me," I said quietly putting the tray down.
"No worries, I'll contact you tonight," she smiled and started eating. I walked back my head in the clouds. My boss just shook his head. Bart gave me a thumbs up. After work I walked outside towards my bike when I got a message.
"Hi Daniel, this is Laurel...maybe we should meet somewhere where there is A) Better food and B) No boss to interrupt our conversation. X – Laurel"
"Hi Laurel, sounds like an excellent idea, how about tomorrow night at the Coffee shop on main street, around 8?"
Her response was immediate.
"Sounds lovely, will see you there :-) x".
I could barely sleep at night. The next day at work I was looking at the clock almost every five minutes but finally I was able to leave. I quickly went home, freshened up and changed

into some nicer clothes and went there. She was waiting outside looking stunning. Then again, she always did. I greeted her and she gave me a kiss on the cheek.

"You're getting red again…" she noted, laughing again. I smiled awkwardly and guided her inside. It was not that busy inside the shop and she choose a table in the corner. The waiter came to ask our order. 5 minutes later two cappuccinos were standing in front of us.

"So you come here often?" I asked realizing how lame it sounded. She however seemed to like the awkwardness.

"No, not that often, actually I have only been here for a couple of weeks," she said. I had already realized this because she definitely had a British accent but I didn't say that.

"So, what made you come here? The wedding?" I asked.

"Yes, well sort of, I was planning on moving from Manchester where I lived and suddenly this wedding came up so I stayed with my cousin and now I am looking for my own place to live," she said.

"So, you like it here?" I asked.

"Well, most things…especially some of the people I met," she said looking me straight in the eyes. We finished our coffees and went outside.

"It was really nice seeing you outside of work," she said.

"Yes, I hope we can do this more often," I said.

"Count on it," she said. She kissed me softly on the lips. We went our own separate ways. Butterflies seemed to have filled my stomach. Over the next week we saw each other every day. Going to get coffee, going to the cinema, going for long walks. We talked and talked, we went to a club to dance and I felt like I was in heaven.

I was at work when she suddenly turned up looking distraught.

"Daniel, I have some bad news…I have to go back to

Manchester," she said.

"But….but that's terrible," I answered.

"Well, actually it's a pretty nice place," Bart interjected. Laurel and I both stared at him. "Okay….exit stage left…" he said moving away.

"Will you be back?" I asked.

"I don't know…probably not, Daniel listen…last week has been great…it's just our timing…could not be worse," she said with tears in her eyes. My boss looked at me and gave me a nod. I nodded back and walked with Laurel outside the store. I took her in my arms.

"It's just not fair is it," I said. "I never believed in love at first sight, a lightning strike at clear skies but now that I met you…"

"I know…but we can keep in contact, call, write, e-mail, skype, this doesn't have to be the end," she said. I nodded but I knew that it would be the end. How often does long distance relationship work?

"When will you leave?"

"Tonight," she said. I nodded and we kissed. We said our good byes and she gave me her address in Manchester, then I went back inside. Bart and my boss were waiting on me.

"So I guess she's it, the one that got away," I said morosely.

"You're an idiot," my boss said.

"What?" I asked.

"You heard him," Bart said. "You're an idiot if you let this one go,"

"What, you want me to fly after her and tell her she needs to come back?!" I asked frustrated. What were they thinking? That this was some kind of romance novel?

"Yes, or you stay there," both of them said in unison. You could see that they practiced this speech.

"But I have my own thing here, work, family," I said.

"If you need me I can fire you...or send you on paid leave for the next two weeks," the boss said.

"You would do that?"

"Daniel...I have seen the way she looks at you and the way you look at her...it's how I felt when I met my wife...if you let her go it will be the biggest mistake you'll ever make," he said. Bart nodded.

"Okay...I will go to Manchester then...I need to pack my suitcase...get a ticket..." I quickly ran outside the restaurant and home. I booked my ticket online and the next day I flew to Manchester. Over there I got into a cab, gave the address that Laurel gave me to the cab driver and he drove me to a large villa just outside of Manchester. The gate was open and lots of black cars were standing there. It was a funeral...so that was the family issue she was talking about. I almost instantly regretted coming here.

He got out of the cab and after paying walked on to the grounds of the villa. It didn't take long to find her. She was dressed in black and looked sad. I just stood a bit away against a tree. A priest was speaking kind words about the man in the grave, from his words he gathered it was her grandfather.

She turned around and saw me. Her jaw dropping. She made her way towards me.

"What on earth are you doing here?!" she asked rather harshly.

"I just couldn't let you go...I just couldn't..." I said. "I know...I should have called. If I had known your grandfather had died I would not have come...I'm sorry..."

She looked at me and then smiled.

"I can't believe you would do that for me," she said giving me a hug.

"Why wouldn't I," I said relieved. "I love you,"

"You're an idiot you know that," she said. "But I'm glad you're my idiot," she continued looking me in the eyes and kissing me.

"And I will always be your idiot if you want me to," I responded feeling my face getting red again. She just nodded and smiled and kissed me again.

Short story 8 – Red Lightning

Caity looked into the mirror at her new suit. A bold red
lightning strike on her black Kevlar vest. Tight pants and large
boots and of course a cape.
She had finally graduated from the Hero academy, two years
after she discovered her powers of being able to electrify her
body. She couldn't actually shoot lightning but she could give
her punches and kicks some extra...kick. And tonight would be
her first night on patrol as a hero. Okay, so her school assigned
mentor...Static Shock, would be with her but still. Her earpiece
crackled.
"Caity here...I mean...Red Lightning," she corrected herself.
"Allonsy!" she heard. Static Shock was a Brit and a big fan of
Doctor Who. "Are you ready for your first patrol? The answer
is yes, meet me outside on the plaza." He said quickly. Static
was a speedster and like many others his speech was very fast.
"Coming," she said putting on her mask. One of the side
effects of her powers was being able to transfer herself
through the electric net. It was almost like teleporting. She
jumped inside her outlet in her bathroom and jumped out of
street light on the plaza. Static was not far away from her and
spotted her immediately.
"Nice suit Red," he said. She smiled feeling her face get a bit
red.
"Thank you Static...yours is nice too," she said looking at his
yellow and blue streamlined leather outfit which he had been
wearing for years.
"I get that a lot," he said. A big smile appeared on his face.
Well, the part that still could be seen behind the mask.
"Now, we just need to wait till we get an alert," he said. He
hadn't even finished his sentence (which is quite a rare

occasion, Caity thought) when the alert went off.

"Okay, got it," Static said. "We're on our way," He nodded to Caity and ran off towards the warehouse where the alert was coming from. Caity jumped in to the lantern and appeared moments later at the warehouse. Static arrived there as well. "You teleporters have all the fun…" he complained softly looking at the building. There was an open window on top. "You'll have to carry me," Caity said. "I can't get there without alerting them," she said. Static nodded and lifted her up, he ran upwards on the building and through the window. He quickly stopped behind a pillar. They both looked leaned against it and looked downwards. Ten men were lifting heavy boxes from the warehouse onto a truck.

"Bit strange time to work don't you think?" Static jokingly asked.

"Well…nowadays it wouldn't be that strange…but I doubt that truck is hired by this company," she replied.

"Good point, okay, I'll blast them from the left, you flank them on the right, please watch yourself," he said. Caity nodded, feeling butterflies in her stomach from excitement. Static disappeared from view and showed up down and started shooting lighting strikes at the criminals. Caity quickly teleported herself down as well and stealthily walked towards a criminal with his back turned to her. She tapped him on the shoulder. He turned around.

"Hi," she said punching him with an electrified fist. He went down in one single punch. A guy close to her turned around as well and made a fist. Luckily her two years at the academy had trained her in close combat. She dodged the punch and kicked him in the side with her electrified foot. When he doubled over she punched him on the top of his head. A third guy had spotted her and aimed his gun at her to then be hit by a lightning strike from Static Shock. She watched the guy drop to the ground when she suddenly felt a kick in her back. She stumbled forward and turned around to see a big guy wearing brass knuckles coming towards her. She electrified both her fists, feet and eyes. The big guy widened his eyes in fear. She punched him square in the jaw and he went down. She heard an applause.

"Well done, Red, well done," Static Shock said looking at the ten men unconscious on the ground. "That trick with your eyes is brilliant, you scared him good,"

"Yeah...but he still got me in the back," she said massaging her back.

"Ah well, that sometimes happens, that's why they give first aid training at the academy," he said. "Ready to file the report,"

Caity nodded. "This is Red Lightning, mission accomplished in Warehouse 84, ten crooks for pick up," she said.

"Acknowledged Red Lightning, thank you for your assistance," a pleasant voice said on the other side.

"You're very welcome" she replied.

"I have another alert coming in if you are ready, Monument Park, a riot,"

"We are on our way," Red lightning said nodding to Static Shock. He nodded back running away at super speed. She jumped in the nearest outlet and made her way towards the park. They arrived around the same time. A big group of rioters were there. It seemed to have been a peaceful protest that changed into a rioting horde. They were kicking down benches and trees.

"What do we do?" Caity asked. These were not criminals... these were people...she couldn't just punch her way to victory here.

"We need to stop them peacefully, I will go talk to them. You stop them from damaging property…without hurting them," Static said. He ran to the fountain the middle of the Park and used a loud speaker that he had built into his costume.

"Citizens! This is Static Shock, hear me! There is no need for this random violence…" Some of the rioters seemed to listen to Static and walked towards the fountain. Others were still busy kicking over benches and trash cans. He walked towards the nearest group.

"Hi," she said awkwardly. "Could you guys please not do this?" she asked. The two guys and a girl looked at her and laughed.

"Who is going to stop us?" the girl asked mockingly. Caity curled her fists and they started to glow as well as her eyes.

"Guess…" she hissed. The trio dropped the trash can they were carrying and put it on the ground.

"You got it…we leave now…ok?" the girl said.

"You do that," Caity said smiling. The trio ran out of the park. Caity turned around and walked towards another group. After about fifteen minutes and without even hitting one single person the rioters had dispersed. She walked towards Static Shock who was setting at the edge of the fountain.

"So, what was the whole protest about?" she asked.

"Something to do with the mayor…they weren't actually very clear about it," Static said. He stood up at the same time Caity heard a strange buzz and suddenly Static fell down, bleeding from his waist.

"What?!" Caity yelled as she ran up to Static looking at his wound.

"Get away…sniper…" Static said softly. Caity looked around and saw two buildings where the shot could have come from, a glint. She quickly jumped into the nearest transformer to the top of the building. She came out of there and looked directly into a rifle.

"I've been watching you," the person who was holding the rifle said. A female wearing body armor.

"Wouldn't it be a shame if Static's new sidekick would die on her first night out?" she mocked.

Caity tried to ignore the taunts.

"You better get back to your mentor...he might die...but do not worry Red Lightning, this is just the start," the woman said. She jumped backwards of the roof. Caity ran to the side and saw that the woman was wearing a jet pack and flying off. She cursed, got her senses together and jumped back to Static Shock.

"Let's get you to a hospital shall we," she said lifting him up. She knew he would recover quicker than normal humans anyway but still.

"So...did you get the sniper?" he asked.

"No...she was aiming the gun at me when I jumped out of the transformer...she knew I was going there...she said she had been watching me...then she jumped of the roof and flew away with a jet-pack,"

"Interesting...looks like you caught the interest of some villain...we'll need to look into that," Static said grunting.

"Yes...but we'll do that after you get better...unlike your favorite show you do not regenerate if you die," she said jokingly. Static laughed. Suddenly she heard a scream.

"Somebody needs a hero, looks like you're it,' Static said.

"But what about you?" Caity asked worried.

"I'll be fine, I can make my way to the hospital, now go," Static said resolutely. Caity nodded and ran towards the scream. As she jumped towards the woman getting robbed at gunpoint she thought to herself that when people would ask her if she could choose not to have her powers would she do it? She

would absolutely not. She punched the robber unconscious and gave the purse back to the woman.
No villain sniper or rioter or robber could persuade her from doing this. Being out here on the streets, helping others that is where she belonged. That's where she felt at home.
That's where she felt like a hero.

Short Story 9 – Pip, the fairy cat

We all know how you can be transported to a Magic Land: mirrors, rabbit holes, wardrobes. What if I told you the Magic land has upgraded. They notice that while mirrors, rabbit holes and wardrobes were still "in use" in 2017 most people were using the cameras on their cellphones, avoiding rabbit holes by staying inside and old fashioned wardrobes were changed to IKEA closets. No respectable magic creature would set foot in a BJÖRN, no sir!
So the magic land had to upgrade, otherwise no more heroes would come and visit them and evil queens, wizards and warlords might take advantage of that. Also, it was bad for tourism.
So they sent out their spies to the normal world and asked them to investigate what humans did nowadays. The reports were depressing. Sitting inside, playing games on a TV called video games, which was strange because according to one of the reports videocassettes had been out of style for almost two decades already and they apparently voted an orangutan as their Lord. The council of the Magic Land decided that they either had to block all ways into Magic Land or that they needed to send a hero to their world to save them.
And although this is a short story, it's not that short so you know that the Magic Council decided to send their own hero. One of the spies had seen a television show where they held a contest to see who the best was in being an artist and the Council wisely decided in their infinite wisdom(I'm totally not forced to write this by the Magic Council...not at all) that this would be the best way to decide who would be the here they seek.
A notice was quickly spread around with 7 words on them: "So

you think you are a hero?"
The response was big. Thousands of would be heroes came to the Magic castle which was in the center of the land. Because they stole the idea of the Never ending story of course although the Council would claim that Never ending story stole it from them in their infinite wisdom (I'm totally not forced to write this by the Magic Council...not at all).
Sadly for us all I don't have time to write about all thousands of would be heroes (big surprise here) so I will tell the story about one of them. His name was Pip, it was short for...well... Pip. He was a a fairy cat. He looked like a cat, moved like a cat, talked like a human and could fly, so he's a fairy cat.
Pip had a black and white fur and a black nose and was rather small for his species and although he always tried to hide his feelings with wit and sarcasm he was a caring fairy cat which was an unusual trait for fairy cats, or cats in general. Normally they are considered pretty selfish. Pip not so much. He was too good to be selfish he said, and humble to, he added.
He had a long way to travel towards the center of the kingdom. Fairy Catland (did I mention, Fairy cats were terrible with creative names) was on the edge of the land. Of all his brothers and sisters he was the only one who wanted to go. The rest were like: Meh...ow...and then started to lick themselves.
Pip shook his head and flew off towards the Magic Castle. Making sure to stop for 16 hours a day in someone's house to play with his own tail, take naps, suddenly sprint from one room to another and beg the house owner for food.
You would think that house owners would find this strange but as fairy cats were a fairly (see what I did there?) common sight to be seen they got used to it and better to give them food before they started singing.

So it took a bit longer than other species of the Magic Land to get there. When he finally got there thousands and thousands of contestants had already been brought before the Council and one was even worse than the others.

There were giants thinking that smashing humans with clubs would be the solution. Elfs who suggested Elven poetry (basically: Yay, trees) would be end of all problems. Vixens who thought they could "vix" the problem with sensual dancing. Dwarves who want to bribe the humans with diamonds, vampires who had a really sucky solution, werewolves who thought crying to the moon in front of the Lords palace would drive him crazy (which the Council briefly considered before brushing it off as not working). A strange creature called a Platypus said he could astonish the humans by producing milk as man from sweating and although the Council agreed that was a cool party trick, it would not help the situation. Fairies who suggested to take people to another magic land to build up a resistance.

Orcs, demons, dragons, goblins, gnomes...all creatures of Magic Land had at least send one of theirs to the Magic Council but none of them fit the bill the Council found. The council was in big distress, they only had one more candidate to go.

"No matter who comes through that door, he or she is it," they decided in their infinite wisdom (I'm totally not forced to write this by the Magic Council...not at all).

Pip walked through the door in the big open theatre where they holding the auditions. The older members of the council weren't even sure if someone had entered.

"Eh...hi," said Pip.

"Hello there, what is your name and species and location of origin," one of the Council members asked in a tired but friendly voice.

"I'm Pip, the fairy cat from Fairycatland," Pip said nervously.

"Welcome Pip, so do you think you can be a hero?"

"I think I can sirs, I'm a fairy cat as I said but I care for these humans. I can make them laugh and forget about the horrible things. I can blend in with them, I look like a normal cat if I can find a human who can help me we can become partners and take over from Lord Orangutan, without anyone knowing I was a fairy cat,"

There were murmurs from the Council.

"Alright Pip, you will be our chosen hero, you better get ready because tomorrow you will go to the land of Humans.

"Thank you, sirs! Thank you so much!" Pip said happily spinning around in the air. He flew outside hitting the door with his face.

"Sorry...that normally doesn't happen..." he said pawing his nose while walking out.

"Are we sure about this?" one Council member asked.

"Don't even start..." another admonished.

The next day, Pip stood ready, with a little backpack on, boots and a hat with feather in front of a large mirror.

The council members were there as well, as were thousands of other beings from Magic land to see their hero save Human land. From the crowd suddenly a scream came and a cat with a Spanish accent walked up to him.

"Give me back my boots, hat and backpack!" he said angrily.

Pip looked around and to the Council members...they nodded.

"Fine..." he said...undressing himself. "Happy now?"

"Yes...' the puss in boots said. "Good luck, amigo!"

"Okay, I'm ready," Pip said feeling his stomach turn.

"Then walk through the mirror,"

Pip walked forward and looked at the Council members.

"Sooo, how do I get back, you know...after I'm done..."
"Well...there is sure some magical wardrobe there you can
use..." one of the Council members said coming forward
picking Pip up. "Now, come on, spit spot!" he said throwing Pip
through the mirror.
"Well, that's that...who's up for a spot of tea?" the other
Council members nodded and walked back to their chambers.
On the other side of the mirror Pip awoke in a box with 6 other
cats. There was a sign which said Free. A little girl and her
mother walked past.
"Oh look mommy, free kittens...can I have one?" she asked.
The mother considered and called her husband on the phone.
"Okay honey, but only one,"
Pip made himself as cute as he could be, which was quite cute.
The girl pointed her finger at him: "I want that one," she said.
"Okay honey, pick him up, see if he likes you," The girl lifted
Pip out of the box. He let her pet him. This human was quite
sweet.
"What are you going to name him," the mother asked.
"Hmmm, good question," she said...she hold Pip in a sort of
hug so his head was on her shoulder.
He whispered: "Pip, call him Pip,"
"Pip...I will call him Pip," the girl said. The mother smiled.
"Okay honey, let's bring Pip home,"
The mother, daughter and Pip crossed the street and stepped
inside a car. Pip looked out of the window. His life as a hero
would start here, he could hardly believe it...something like
that would only happen in a fairy tale.

Short story 10 – Caught Red handed

It was a day like any other day in this small town. The horses were standing patiently at their troughs, the blacksmith was outside hammering on a horse shoe. Sheriff Joe Coltrane smiled as he stepped outside his office hands on his gun belt in a relaxed fashion. Today so far looked like a perfect, calm day.

He lighted a cigarette and walked towards the doctor's office. The good old doctor was inside reading a book but gave a short wave when he saw the sheriff through the window. The sheriff waved back and walked towards the general store. He needed to buy some nails anyway for some repairs at home. He walked inside. The old Madam Carpenter was standing behind her till as usual.

"Good morning sheriff, how may I be of service?" she asked kindly with her thick southern accent.

"Good morning Madam Carpenter, do you have some 20 mm nails in stock?" he asked looking around to see what other new wares she might have gotten.

"I think I do," she said moving from her till to a big closet on the other side of the room. In there she kept all kinds of nails, screws and thingamabobs you could ever need for hammering, screwing or mounting things on top of other things. After only a moment of searching she said.

"There ya go," and she gave him a small box.

"Thank you, how much…"

"Oh don't bother," she said smiling.

"Well…that is very kind of you madam," he said tipping his hat. He put the box in his pocket and walked outside. The sun was rising and he felt it getting warmer. He smiled as he walked further on his morning patrol. He greeted the farmers who were already working before the sun was even up and asked them if they had spotted anything weird. Luckily they didn't. He made his way back to the center of town to provide his morning report to Mayor Brimstein, which he did every morning. Mrs. Brimstein made the best coffee in the whole town, when suddenly three strangers on horses arrived there as well. Joe turned toward them, noting they were all armed with guns and knives.

"Howdy strangers," he said. "What brings you to this small part of the land?" he asked casually.

The biggest stranger looked at him and smiled a crooked smiled.

"We are just passing through, traveled all night so we want to water our horses and ourselves before we go on further,"

That sounded innocent enough. "Ah, very well, the saloon is further along the road and there you can water your horses as well," he said pointing with his finger behind him.

"Much obliged Sheriff," the stranger said. He nodded to the other two men and they left towards the saloon.

Joe turned towards the Mayor's house and went inside. The servant greeted him and guided him towards the office.

"Good morning Joe,"

"Jack," Joe said tipping his head and taking it off. He looked to his left where Mrs. Brimstein, Clarice, was standing.

"Clarice," he said. She smiled.

"Any news to report?" she asked putting down the tray with coffee.

"Nothing much, three armed strangers just arrived. Said they were looking to rest a bit before moving onward. I pointed them to the saloon," he said. "Other than that...nothing," he said.

"Three strangers huh?" Jack said stroking his beard. "Hmmm,

we just got this message from Hub city, warning about three men," He produced a piece of paper from his pocket and handed it to Joe. On it were three photos. Photos of the men he just pointed to the saloon.

"Oh god…" Joe said. He stood up. "Those are those men, I need to go,"

"Wait…there is more, a bounty hunter is hunting them…here," he gave him another photo.

"I haven't seen him yet…if I see him I will ask him for assistance, I need to inform Deputy Jones," Joe said. He hurried out of the office and out of the house back to the Sheriff's station.

"Will! Where ever you are, you're needed, now!" he shouted.

"I'm here…" a young man looking slightly hungover walked out of the office.

"We have three dangerous men at the saloon. We are going to stop them, are you ready?" Joe said. This seems to awaken Will a bit.

"Of course, let's go!" he said tucking in his shirt, fastening his gun belt. They made their way to the saloon when they saw a man on a horse arriving. It was the bounty hunter of the photo the mayor had shown him. The bounty hunter looked intense. He was still pretty young but had a big scar on his face. The Sheriff walked up to him.

"Bounty hunter, I am Sheriff Coltrane, this is my deputy Will Jones, we know you are hunting three men that are inside the saloon, we are doing the same. Let's join forces," he said formally.

The bounty hunter looked at him and smiled.

"Well, I suppose I should say no, say I work alone and all that crap but I would actually welcome the help," he said. He sounded like he hadn't spoken for a while. "The name's Red, nice to meet you Sheriff, deputy," he continued.

"Good, so you know these guys better than us, any suggestions?"

"They will have started drinking as soon as they got here, their first target will be the cash in the saloon, after that they will try and rob the local bank. They will shoot anyone who even suggests trying to block them. I haven't heard any gun shots while I was here so that's good," he hadn't even finished his sentence when a shot was heard.

"I should not have said that..." he said. "Okay, Sheriff, you and me at the door, Deputy Jones, go around the back and attack them from the flank. Don't start shooting until we do," Red said.

"Ex-military?" the Sheriff asked. Red nodded. They drew their guns and quickly made their way to the entrance of the bar. They took cover at the walls and peaked inside. The shot that was fired seem to have gone into the ceiling. The bartender was opening his till with shaking hands. All three of them had their guns aimed at him.

"This is Sheriff Joe Coltrane, surrender now or we have no choice but to open fire!" Joe said. The three men turned around in unison and without waiting they kicked over two tables and took cover behind it.

"Well...so much for the peaceful option," Red noted. He peaked around the corner and shot. Instantly the shots got returned. The Sheriff also fired back, not betting on actually hitting anything.

Suddenly another shot was heard and a loud scream.

"Good shot Will!" the Sherriff thought. One of the three men had fallen down. The other two quickly ran to another table to find cover. Joe and Red made their old cover their new cover and Will joined them.

Will checked the bandit that he shot, he was dead.

"Well...there goes your alive bounty Mister Red," he said.

"I'll live," Red noted looking at the other side of the room. Shots came from that side and he quickly hid back inside cover.

"Well...this stinks," Will noted. "What do we do now?"

Joe looked over the edge of the flipped table and saw that the two bandits were very close to the bar, on which stood load of alcohol.

"I have an idea...we douse them in alcohol and set them on fire...it won't kill them but it will get them out of cover for sure," he said. Red nodded. The three of them aimed their guns at the bottles above the heads of the bandits and shot their guns empty. The alcohol was pouring downwards on the bandits. Before they could respond Joe lighted a match and threw it at them. It worked like a charm. The bandits were lit on fire and jumped up trying to douse the flames and dropping their guns. Joe, Will and Red guided them to the water troughs and dumped them in it.

"Gents, you are hereby under arrest," Joe said to them once they got out of the water. He cuffed them and brought them to the Sheriff's station and locked them in jail. He went outside where Red was standing smoking a cigarette. The sheriff leaned against the railing.

"Thanks for your help Red," he said. "I do not necessarily agree with bounty hunting but it is good that these guys are locked away, you have earned it,"

"Thank you sheriff and might I say you do a mighty good job in this town to keep it safe, if more sheriff's would work like you I think I might not be needing to bounty hunt," Red said tipping his hat.

"You do what you have to do," Joe simply said. "So, what

now?"
"I'll collect my bounty and see what other bandits need to be caught…"red handed" he joked. He climbed on his horse.
"Let's hope that if we meet next time we can actually have a drink at the saloon," he continued.
"That's a promise," Joe said tipping his hat. Red spurred his horse and they drove off in the setting sun.
It was a day like any other day in this small town. The horses were standing patiently at their troughs, the blacksmith was outside hammering on a horse shoe. Sheriff Joe Coltrane smiled as he stepped inside his office hands on his gun belt in a relaxed fashion. Today had been a perfect, calm day…mostly.

Short story 11 – Fear us!

Stephen and Ashley stepped out of the bus and looked
towards the gray building in front of them. Other people were
following him from the bus as well.
"Well, that is definitely not what they showed in the
brochure," Ashley said.
"No...definitely not," Stephen said to his best friend for years
now. A middle aged man was waiting for them on top of the
stairs leading to the building. The whole group gathered in
front of him.
"Welcome all! Welcome all!" he said smiling. "Welcome to this
extraordinary fair where there will be lectures given by all
kinds of experts in all kinds of fields. We have scientists,
writers, singers and actors who will all tell you about their
expertise!"
Stephen and Ashley looked at each other excited.
"You will be divided by what you signed up for and assigned a
color, you will even get our custom colored shirts so you can
recognize other people in your group," the man continued.
"This way you will always know where to go and what time
according to the schedule you have and on the screens in and
around the building,"
For the Science fair, you will get assigned the color red, please
come when I call your name. This was what Stephen and
Ashley signed up for. Their group consisted of 9 people,
including the interpreter for Brett, who was deaf.
"Boy, she is going to have a hard time to next few days," Ashley
noted...
We got assigned another person of the event organization who
brought us to our wing where we would stay. Every person got
their own room assigned. Stephen and Ashley had rooms

opposite each other. In each room there was a single bed, a small closet, and a small bathroom. The bed was comfortable. He changed his shirt to the red one they provided and looked at the schedule. First lecture would be in an hour already. He crossed over to Ashley's room and knocked on the door.

"Ready Ash?" he asked. She opened the door wearing her red shirt

"Hell yeah, let's explore!" Ashley said. They walked out of their dormitory and to the main hall. Other people were walking around with green shirts, blue shirts, yellow shirts and other red shirts.

"Funny, how they gave us the science geeks the red shirts," Ashley said.

"I guess someone in that committee is a fan of Star Trek," Stephen joked. They checked the map to make sure that they knew were they needed to go for their first lecture and then went outside. They had driven 5 hours to get to this school and it was just one hour in the afternoon. The building where they stayed might have been looking old and decrepit but the surrounding grounds looked lovely. Green fields, a forest surrounding it and a big lake. They walked around the building which looked oddly rectangular from all sides. They couldn't totally go around as it was blocked by a hedge and a fence. It said that behind it were the vegetable gardens and that for a tour they needed to fill in an application. They walked towards the lake.

"No fishing or swimming allowed" a sign said.

"Well, good thing I'm not that into swimming or fishing anyway," Stephen said. Ashley nodded.

"With these schedules I wonder when anyone ever has time for that," she said. "I mean, today we are finished at 6 and tomorrow morning first lecture is at 8. And I thought that this would be like a holiday," she sighed.

"Well, we won't have homework, so that's good, speaking of, it's time," he said. They went back inside not noticing that the man who had greeted them when they got out of the bus was watching them from a second floor window.

The first lecture was given by a famous biologist and the class was full of other people with red shirts as well, brought in by other buses from all over the country that same day. The lecture was about evolution and the controversy around the word theory. They both had heard of it before watching videos on YouTube and all but still interesting. There was also time for a Q&A. The second lecture was after a short break about astrophysics. Both of them did study some physics in high school but weren't that knowledgeable. Luckily for them this lecture series was made for the layman and this whole fair was intended for people who were just interested in these topics. The last lecture of today was about the history of scientific discovery. From Newton, to Galileo, to Marie Curie and Einstein.

They went to have dinner in a big mess hall where all four colors were united. Although there were no set rules on which table you could sit the colors stayed separated pretty much. Stephen wondered if that was on purpose.

"It's almost like they put us in houses like in Harry Potter," he said.

"Yeah, well...good thing we are Gryffindor then," Ashley joked. They ate a simple but tasty meal and went outside after. It was early in the night now.

"I heard they have an excellent library in this building, shall we go check it out," Ashley suggested.

"A library...sure...exciting..." Stephen said sarcastically.

"Are you mocking books? Cause it sound like you are mocking

books right now?!" she said veining anger.

"Me? Never!" Stephen said veining shock. "Why don't we take a walk around the lake and after that we can visit this precious library of yours, Hermione," he continued. She narrowed her eyes and punched him in the shoulder.

Stephen laughed and ran away around the lake. Ashley ran after him. The lake was not that big but was surrounded by trees as well. Ashley had brought her binoculars with her. There were some birds on the lake but not much else. They set down on the opposite of the school building.

"I wish I had brought my camera, from here the building doesn't look so ghastly," Stephen said. Ashley was hardly listening. Stephen tapped her shoulder.

"Eh, earth to Ash," he said.

"I heard you..." she said.

"What's wrong?" Stephen asked.

"We are being watched," she said giving him the binoculars. "Second floor, third window from the right,"

Stephen moved checked the third window. The guy who greeted them was indeed looking out the window and in their direction but clearly, how could he see them without binoculars.

He zoomed in on the guy when suddenly the guy was directly looking at him and giving him an evil smile and wink.

"What the..." Stephen said dropping the binoculars.

"What? What happened?" Ashley asked.

"The guy smiled and winked at me...he knew I was watching him," Stephen said.

"Now....that's impossible...how could he know?" Ashley said.

"I don't know...but I'm not going to ask...I think we need to get out of here"

"Eh how? We are at least an hour away with a car from any

town or city, let alone from home, I don't know if you checked but I don't have any cell coverage here,"
"I don't know...let's go to my room...maybe I have...maybe this is all a sick joke..."
They made their way back to their dormitory, it was getting dark. They went into Stephen's room. He quickly locked the door and threw his bag on the bed. He got out his cellphone. As they both expected there was no connection here.
They sat on the bed.
"Okay...we should calm down...think rational...I could just have imagined it and there might be nothing strange here," he said.
"Yes...just your imagination...sounds good...let's go for that one," Ashley said not sounding so sure. She got up and walked to the door when suddenly the doorknob was rattled. Ashley jumped backwards falling down. Stephen caught her just in time and helped her up.
From the outside the voice of the man who was watching them came.
"I don't know if this was explicitly told earlier but the organization would prefer it if members of the opposite sex would stay out of each others rooms for the duration of the fair...you know...just to prevent unwanted...complications.
"How do you even know there are two people here?" Stephen asked.
"Come now Stephen...can I call you Stephen? People saw you and Miss Ashley walking inside and the door is locked. I was once a young man too you know," he said.
"And why would the head of this organization care so much about what two young people are doing?" Ashley asked.
Suddenly the man stepped through the door, not opening the door and stepping through the hole, but through the door itself.

"Well, that is quite an interesting question, you two fascinate me, I have been keeping my eye on you for since you arrived here, as you may noticed,"

Stephen and Ashley nodded.

"We have, what do you want?" Stephen asked a lot more bravely than he felt.

"For you to join us," he said. His eyes were glowing red. "It gets so terribly boring here after 300 years of being alone," he said. "We need some fresh blood that can stay alive...the dead bodies we have enough in the lake," he casually continued. The two of them looked in horror.

"Yes...that is why we organize these fun for everyone fairs...to get food for us in a safe and controlled manners," he laughed, they could now see that his whole mouth was full of razor sharp teeth. The man had transformed into a creature with leathery wings and a sharp beak with teeth and red eyes.

"I'm sorry," Stephen said "But. Not. Interested," he continued throwing his bag at the creature seeing it went right through the creature. Their room was on the lowest floor. He picked up the cupboard next to his desk and threw it through the window.

"Come on Ash!" he shouted. The both of them jumped out of the window and landed. They ran to the road.

"Great plan Stephen, what now?!" Ashley yelled.

"We run for it...I don't think that they want to go far from this building..." he said. They ran southwards back from where the bus had brought them. When suddenly three of these leathery bird beings flew out of the windows and followed them.

"Three?! Now, that's just not fair..." Stephen said. They kept running but the creatures were faster.

"You cannot escape!" one of the creatures said.

"Surrender now and we will make you suffer less," another

one echoed.

"Yeah…don't worry, it only hurts a little bit," the third one said.

Ashley threw the binoculars she had around her neck towards one of the creatures and it went right through it.

"These creatures are intangible….we can't hit them!" Stephen said.

"So…if we can't hit them…can they hit us?" Ashley asked, she stopped in her tracks. Stephen stopped as well.

The three creatures also stopped.

"They apparently can't…" Stephen said looking at them. "Can you?!" he challenged them.

"Maybe we can't! But there is so much more we can do! You should fear us!" one of them said flying towards Stephen. Stephen didn't even blink when the creature flew right through him.

"You feed on fear…you need people to be afraid," Stephen said. Ashley nodded.

"And without that fear…you don't exist!" she continued.

Uttering that last word seem to shock the three creatures who suddenly disappeared.

"So…do you think that there is a whole lake of dead bodies out there?" Stephen asked while they walked back towards the house.

"I don't know…and I don't wanna find out,"

"Well…that is very unHermione of you, Hermione," he said.

Ashley narrowed her eyes again but before she could punch him he was already running back to the school.

Short story 12 – Tick, tock

Tick, tock
Tick, tock
Ten dead girls walking around a clock
Tick, tock
Tick, tock
Ten dead girls running around a clock
Tick, tock
Tick, tock
Ten dead girls dancing around a clock
Tick, tock
Tick, tock
Ten dead girls skipping around a clock
Tick, tock
Tick, tock
Ten dead girls singing around a clock
Tick, tock
Tick, tock
Ten dead girls crying around a clock

"Joffrey! It's time!" his mother shouted from the kitchen.
Joffrey woke up and climbed out of his bed.
"Coming, mother!" he shouted down.
"Good, hurry up! We're almost too late," she replied. He
quickly dressed himself in his Sunday best and went down. His
mother was there waiting and both went outside their little
hut. The rest of the small village near a giant castle was also
walking up towards it.
The king was almost back home from a long and distant war.
The news had come last night that the king would arrive soon.
Now the whole village was waiting to see a glimpse of the king

and maybe some of the treasures he had brought with him. The palace guards had put barriers up so that they couldn't get close to the king. Joffrey smiled though, this would be the first time in his life he would see the king. The king left 10 years ago, just as Joffrey was born. Today was his birthday and having the king back, which according to his mother was a noble man, was an excellent way to start his birthday.
He and his mother gathered near to a barrier and from afar they could see a big group of horse riders coming this way. It were the knights, they had shining armor and horses. They smiled and waved to the onlookers. The onlookers were shouting their names. Then a big coach with gold decorations drove past and the king looked out of the window and waved. Joffrey stood on the barrier and waved as well. Then he accidentally tumbled forward and fell hard on the ground.
"Joffrey!" his mother yelled worried. A palace guard walked up to him.
"You okay, son?" he asked politely enough. Joffrey tried to get up but his head was spinning around. Suddenly another male voice said something.
"Put the boy and his mother in my coach, we will let the doctor take a look at him,"
"M'lord?"
"You heard me," the king said.
"Of course, my lord," the guard said. He gently picked up Joffrey and put him in the coach, laying him down on one of the seats. A moment later Joffrey's mother sat next to him.
"My lord...I cannot express in words..." his mother stammered.
"Then don't," the king said kindly. "What is your name, mrs?"
"Martha, sire and my son's name is Joffrey," she said.
"And the boy's father?"
"He died, 9 years ago" she said.

"I am sorry to hear that," the King said meaning it. They drove up to the castle. Joffrey's headache got even worse.

One of the guards picked him up and quickly brought him to a big room with lots of strange bottles and devices in it. An old man with a big white beard walked towards the guard.

"Ah, this is the boy I've heard so much about, can you put him on that bed?" he said. The guard brought him to the bed.

"The king wants to see the boy as soon as he can walk again," the guard said.

"Of course...of course..." the older man said. The guard quickly turned around and left the room.

"Now, let's see if we can fix that wound if yours," the man said smiling taking a warm wet towel out of a bowl with water and cleaning the wound.

About 15 minutes later Joffrey's wound had been dressed and the man had given him something to drink against the headache.

"Now, be careful out there and have your mother clean the bandage every day okay?"

"Yes of course, sir, thank you sir," he said bowing.

"That's okay, just remember those manners when you go see the king, the guard outside will take you there," the man said smiling. Joffrey smiled back and walked outside where a guard was waiting.

"Follow me," he said. Joffrey had a bit of a hard time keeping up with the guard but soon they arrived in the big throne room. The king was sitting at the end with his mother sitting in another seat on the side.

"Ah, it's good to see you walking around again son," the king said smiling. Joffrey walked up to him and kneeled down.

"Thank you my lord for taking care of me," he said.

"That's all good, son," the king said. "Please stand up,"

Joffrey did so.

"So, your mother and I have been talking and to repay me for the service I did for you we agreed it would be a good idea for you and your mother to stay and work in the castle, unless of course you can think of a better way to repay me?" the king said casually with a slight smile. Joffrey was feeling lightheaded again. Living in the castle? That was a dream that come true.

"No my lord...I wouldn't know...thank you my lord...anything of course..." he stumbled. His mother beamed at him.

"Then that's settled. I have my guards gathering your personal belongings, your first task will be to clean up some of the things I have collected from my travels," the king said. It was a dismissal. The next few days seemed to go very fast as the gains from the war were slowly brought in. On the tenth day an old clock was brought in. It was very dirty and with wood polish and rags Joffrey started cleaning the clock. He started on the top and noticed that in golden letters something was written there.

Tick, tock

He started cleaning faster and below the words more words appeared.

Tick, tock

He continued cleaning and more words appeared.
Ten dead girls walking around the clock
A shiver went up his spine. Out of morbid curiosity he cleaned the whole side of the clock and a poem appeared:

Tick, tock
Tick, tock
Ten dead girls walking around a clock
Tick, tock
Tick, tock
Ten dead girls running around a clock
Tick, tock
Tick, tock
Ten dead girls dancing around a clock
Tick, tock
Tick, tock
Ten dead girls skipping around a clock
Tick, tock
Tick, tock
Ten dead girls singing around a clock
Tick, tock
Tick, tock
Ten dead girls crying around a clock

He stood up and walked outside the room.
"Guard...there is something the king must see, please get him,"
he said.
"You better make sure it's something worthwhile, kid," the
guard said.
Five minutes later the king arrived with the Joffrey's mother.
"What do you have to show me boy?" the king asked kindly.
"My lord, I was cleaning the old clock you brought here and it
has a message on it, or a poem, I thought you would be
interested to see it," he said bowing deep.
"Interesting, well, show it to me then," the king said. The three
of them walked inside the room where the clock was. The king
read the poem.

"Well...that's rather dreadful...but I have heard this poem
before, during the war...we should have a list where this is
from right?"
"Yes, my lord, it's right here," Joffrey said giving the king the
list.
"Ah yes, here it is...we had just freed this village when we saw
a group of girls at a school dancing around pole chanting this
rhyme, rather creepy, I would guess they learned it from here,"
"I wonder what it means," Martha said.
"Probably nothing, just some old folktale which got lost
somewhere through the ages," the King said dismissively.
"Either way, it's an interesting find, lad, good work,"
"Thank you my lord," Joffrey said bowing down again. The king
and his mother left and Joffrey went on cleaning the clock
reciting the poem in his head.

Tick, tock
Tick, tock
Ten dead girls walking around a clock...

The whole day the poem was stuck in his head, during dinner,
during the evening when the king was telling his stories about
the war. When he went to his bed in chambers he felt like he
could hear the voices of girls chanting.
He lay on the bed and tried to go sleep. When suddenly he felt
a cold wind. He opened his eyes seeing ten pale girls dancing
around his bed chanting:

Tick, tock
Tick, tock
Ten dead girls walking around a clock
Tick, tock

Tick, tock
Ten dead girls running around a clock
Tick, tock
Tick, tock
Ten dead girls dancing around a clock
Tick, tock
Tick, tock
Ten dead girls skipping around a clock
Tick, tock
Tick, tock
Ten dead girls singing around a clock
Tick, tock
Tick, tock
Ten dead girls crying around a clock

He screamed.
His mother came running through the door to find the bed
empty. She rushed outside of her room and screamed for help.
The guards came and while she explained that her son had
disappeared a search party was started including the king. He
and Martha finally ended up at her son's workplace where the
clock was still standing. She walked towards and read the
poem till the end when she suddenly screamed again, an extra
verse had been added in gold letters.

Tick, tock
Tick, tock

A poor dead boy crying around a clock

Short story 13 – Cold discovery

"What was I thinking?!" I said out loud towards the snow. Instead of getting an answer I got a mouth full of snow. I should have known it too. I was trained for this. I walked further and after a back breaking 15 minute walk I reached the base. I quickly opened the door and went inside.
"Doctor Black, welcome back," Sergeant Montgomery said.
"Yes, that one never gets old," I noted while taking of my hat, glasses and scarf.
"Argh…you're ice cold man, ice cold," he continued.
"Ice puns? Really?" I asked incredulous. I took of my jacket, snow trousers and boots and put them back in my locker.
"Anyway, did you find anything?" Montgomery asked more seriously.
"Sadly no," I said sitting down at the table opening my laptop. I opened up a map of the area, which unsurprisingly was white, but with the markers we put down we could pinpoint on the screen where we have searched. "But I would have been surprised if we found something every day," I continued. The sergeant sat down next to me looking at the screen.
"Seems to me it should be a lot easier if we would comb the area," he suggested. I shook my head.
"Well, if we had enough man I would maybe consider it but A) We don't and B) That's dangerous, you run the risk of damaging the artifacts," I said.
"I am sure we could teach the men to be careful with them," Montgomery said defensively. I nodded and gave him a reassuring pat on the shoulder.
"I am not questioning the skills of your troops Sergeant, they have proven themselves more than worthy," I said.
"Well thank you doctor, I'm sure our CO at the home base will

love to hear that in your next report," Montgomery said. "Can I bring you some coffee?" he continued.

"If you could?" I said. My eyes focused back on the screen. The marker I dropped at the place I investigated lighted up.

"Good...it means I don't have to go back there,"

I opened my daily report file and started typing when someone poked me in the shoulder.

"Last word?" a female said.

"Snow," I said.

"Wow...of all the things you can report on you are reporting on the snow...and that's where the taxpayers are paying millions of dollars for?"

"Well, Hailey, what were your reports about?" I said jokingly raising my eyebrow. I looked at her.

"Snow..." she said with a resigned sigh. "So, nothing new in this sector either?" she asked pointing to the place I just came from.

"Sadly no, tomorrow a new chance in the sector next to it," I said.

"If there is anything at all," she said. "We have been here for three weeks and still nothing,"

"Don't be so negative, we have found one here, that means there is more...it's not possible for only thing to be here... unless you are suggesting that an explorer of 1000 years ago of another continent was exploring Antarctica and died here leaving only his spearpoint..."

"Yeah yeah...I get it," she said impatiently. "Let's go together tomorrow, we will be done quicker," she said.

"We'll go with the whole group," Montgomery said walking in with coffee. "The place that is on the plan for tomorrow requires ice climbing and some other rough terrain, it will be safer if we go all,"

"I trust your assessment Sergeant, then let's go sleep early so we can leave at dawn tomorrow," I said closing my laptop. The sergeant nodded and after coffee and dinner we all went to our bunks. I regretted my plan of getting up early as soon as my alarm went off. 15 minutes later two tired archaeologists and five army men who were a lot more awake were drinking coffee and having breakfast.

We got dressed in our protective clothing and the Sergeant gave last minute instructions to the squad. Then we left our little base camp. Luckily the storm of last night was over and it was clear. That made the travel a lot easier. Using the computer that was attached to my arm I was able to determine which way to go. We walked for about an hour when they reached a cliff where they had to climb up. We divided ourselves in two teams with Hailey and two of the army men in our team and Montgomery and the others in the other team and started our long climb up. We tethered ourselves to each other and put new anchors every time we climbed up a bit. It was a very slow process. The team of soldiers was ahead of us naturally but luckily it wasn't a race. It was almost midday when we finally arrived on the top.

We quickly made a camp with a bit of shelter so we could sit.

"That was a nice climb, wasn't it?" Montgomery said.

"Could be worse I suppose," I answered drinking coffee from a thermos mug. : Luckily we are almost there and no more cliffs to climb, except later when we go back,"

"Shouldn't be as much of a problem," Hailey suggested. Both of us nodded. We packed everything in again and set for the last leg of our journey. It wasn't far. We first put down our marker. Then I used a long drill I had and made a whole in the ice. I did this four times more when suddenly I heard a clang.

"What?!" I shouted.

"What's wrong?" Hailey asked.

"I heard something, as if I was hitting metal," I said. I dug into my bag and got out a flexible camera. I put in the hole and watched the life feed on my computer. It went down and then it hit something gray.

"Definitely metal," I said. Hailey nodded.

"Sergeant, we found something, we need the power tools!" Hailey shouted. An hour later the ice on top of the metal was removed. It looked like a metal plate. No, it looked like

"A hatch?" Montgomery suggested.

"How on earth is there a hatch here?" I wondered out loud. Hailey pulled on it and it opened surprisingly easy. We all shined our lights down but we could only see a ladder.

"Well...down we go..." I said. I climbed down the ladder. It was long and I noticed that it was getting warmer and warmer. When we finally reached the bottom of the stairs we took of our winter gear. There was only one way to go from the bottom of the ladder so we went there. The soldiers took lead with their weapons aimed. I didn't know what to expect, such an elaborate cave system here? Who made it, when was it made? There were no signs or drawings or anything on the wall. After a while the corridor widened and we came into a big circular room.

"Wow...this must have been dug out a millennia ago!" Hailey exclaimed. She looked around. There were some skeletons around and a big pedestal in the middle of the room. My eyes were more focused on the big ring that was made on one edge of the room. It looked like some sort of gateway. Hailey was looking at one of the skeletons.

"Marshall, look at this," she said. I turned to her and she was holding up from what it looked like a spear.

"It's the same type that was found before, but look at how this

person was dressed," she said. I looked at the skeleton.
"That looks like Amazonian clothing...but how..." I wondered.
Then suddenly they heard a loud "THUD" from behind them.
They turned around. One of the soldiers had pressed a stone
on the pedestal and it gave light.
"What on earth..."
Suddenly the symbols on the ring started to light up as well
and a weird shimmery puddle like layer came to existence. In it
they could see a temple, a luscious forest and even the sun.
"This must be the way those soldiers came here...it's some
kind of teleportation device," Montgomery said.
"But how?" I said.
"What does it matter...it's incredible..." Hailey said. She walked
towards the puddle.
"Don't!" I said but it was too late, Hailey had walked through it
and was now on the other side. They could see her but not
hear her. I walked after her also through the puddle. I
immediately felt the warmth of the sun on my skin. The
soldiers and Montgomery also followed through. I looked back
and saw that on this side the puddle wasn't see through. It
then disappeared.
"This is incredible!" Montgomery said.
"Yeah, it's pretty amazing," I checked my computer to see if
the satellites had already picked up our location but nothing.
"Eh...not that I want to worry anyone but I don't see a return
pedestal here," Hailey said.
"I'm also not getting any data from the satellites," I said.
"Probably nothing," Montgomery said calmly. "We'll find this
pedes..." suddenly he was interrupted when an arrow hit him
in the chest. He fell down dead.
"Quick, hide!" one of the soldiers said.
"There shouldn't be anyone here...most old Amazonian tribes

are extinct..." I said.

"Marshall! Look at them! Those are not old Amazonian tribes and we are not on earth!"

"What do you mean we are not on earth?" I asked.

"Look up! Since when does the Earth has two suns?" I looked up and indeed two bright yellow stars were in the sky.

Short story 14 – Abel and Roderick

Once upon a time in a land far far away from here there were
story tellers. Story tellers had an important job. They told the
fairy tales, the legends, and the fables to the people so that
those people could have dreams and hope and something to
aspire too. Story tellers were a mysterious folk. Coming out of
nowhere and disappearing soon after they wowed their
audience with their tall tales.
Nobody knew that the stories were real, which they couldn't
because it happened once upon a time, in a land far far away
from here...
"Come on Abel! Keep up!" Sir Roderick exclaimed while riding
on a horse towards a band of bandits. Abel ran after the horse
with his notepad in hand and a feather pencil in the other. The
ink he had tied on his hat.
"Be a story teller Abel, people will pay you well for that Abel,
it's a glorious job, Abel," he said to himself in a mocking voice.
"Coming Sir!" he yelled after the Knight in blinding armor. The
sunlight hit hard on the silvery metal and reflected the light
towards the bandits. Abel was close enough and set down. He
quickly dipped his feather in ink and started to write the
actions of Sir Roderick.
"And he jumped of the horse with his sword in both hands and
stabbed the last of the bandits through the chest," he finished
his last sentence. "And the crowd went wild..." he softly said,
got up from where he sat and walked towards Sir Roderick.
"Excellent work sir," he said. Sir Roderick stood up.
"As expected of course, now turn around Abel," he said. Abel
knew what would come now. "Sir" Roderick would now loot
the bodies claiming all valuable items but that of course could
not be written down. As if he turning around would make the

difference.

"Calm down Abel, you are only here to record, not judge," Abel said to himself. He looked at the sky while Sir Roderick did his business.

"Okay Abel! Time to go!" he said. He was already on his horse and walking away. Abel shook his head and quickly followed him. They went to a nearby village where the people received the knight in a hero's welcome. Abel had to dodge a couple of villagers. They went to the local inn and Sir Roderick started his second hobby after looting, drinking and have women fawning over him. Abel felt sick in his stomach. He wrote the shortest paragraph possible about this and went to his own little room. He decided that the king really must have hated him to give him such a miserable job. Or maybe the king didn't know better, after all, all the stories about Sir Roderick were positive. He was basically a bad guy with very good PR.

"That should be the name of his biography," Abel joked to himself. He fell asleep soon after but was rudely awakened early in the morning by Roderick.

"Abel! We need to go, there is an old castle nearby with a dragon and I want to leave here before they ask me to take care of it," Roderick said. He clearly was half drunk.

"What on earth are you talking about?" Abel asked half asleep.

"I don't care much for dragons..." Roderick said looking shiftily around.

"You are afraid of dragons?" Abel asked.

"How dare you say that?!" Roderick asked angrily but his hands were shaking. "Let's get out of here before people realize I'm still here and ask me to kill the dragon..." he continued.

"Alright, alright..." Abel said a devious plan coming up in his head. He quickly gathered his bag and together they made it downstairs, people there were drunkenly asleep, even the barkeep was napping on his counter. Abel then stuck his foot out and Roderick tripped and fell against the counter.

"Look who's here! Sir Roderick!" Abel yelled, quickly hiding behind the door. The people were suddenly very awake and interested in where he was going.

Abel called out from behind the door with a high pitched voice to hide his own.

"Surely, Sir Roderick you aren't going to try to defeat the dragon at the old castle?"

Sir Roderick looked around worried.

"Come on Sir Roderick," came from the crowd. Quickly the whole bar was cheering him on. Sir Roderick waved with his arms motioning for silence.

"Okay, okay…okay…I will take of this dragon problem for you," he said reluctantly. He turned around and walked out.

"Abel!" he shouted. Abel stopped laughing behind the door. He had totally forgotten he had to go with him…to the dragon. He used every curse word he knew and then some in his head and followed the knight outside.

Together they made it to the old castle about two kilometers away from the village.

"Okay…so here we are…" Sir Roderick said quietly. It was hard for Abel to not feel sorry for the knight and for himself.

"Yeah…my lord…I am going to find a good space to eh…keep watch on the proceedings," Abel said.

"Yeah…yeah…you do that…" Sir Roderick said, staring at the decrepit building. "We don't want you to miss anything right? Got to write about my heroic deeds right,"

"Indeed my lord, you'll do fine I'm sure of it," Abel said trying to comfort the knight who really looked scared. Abel walked up to a hill not far from the castle and could see in on the main plaza. Roderick had approached the castle and drawn his sword and shield. He entered it disappearing from view and appearing a couple seconds later on the plaza. No dragon in sight yet.

After an hour of nothing happening Abel was getting bored and climbed down the hill and went to the castle. Inside he saw that Roderick was just standing there. He had put his sword on the ground.

"Well...this is pretty anti-climactic..." Roderick said, not looking like he minded it. "You better skip this part,"

"Yeah...don't worry about it..." Abel said. Suddenly a loud rumble came from within the castle.

"What was that?!" Roderick exclaimed quickly picking up his sword.

"Three guesses! First two don't count!" Abel said quickly running towards a stair case on the far side of the castle. He ran up 5 flights upstairs and ended up in the North tower. He looked down and saw that the dragon had come out of the castles. His scales were black as the night and purple smoke was coming out of his nostrils. He walked on two giant legs which ended in humongous claws. His arms were muscular and ended in claws as well. His wings where made from leather. Sir Roderick had apparently been able to gather enough courage to look the beast directly in his jade eyes. A purple flame shot out of the dragon's mouth. Roderick put his shield up and it deflected the blast. The dragon gave an angry roar and tried to claw the knight with all his might.

Sir Roderick dodged it with surprising agility and slashed with his sword to the hind legs of the beast. It got deflected on the scales. Abel saw that although the knight was fighting valiantly he could never win from this beast with his sword alone.

He thought of how much he hated the knight and how with

this dragon he could finally become the story teller of a real hero, not some loser like Sir Roderick. But...it was his fault that Roderick was here. Roderick, bastard as he was did not want to fight the dragon but whether he only cared for his ego or changed his mind because of the villagers' request. He was here to fight the dragon, he also didn't run when he had the chance. Maybe...just maybe, Sir Roderick was not that bad of a guy after all.

There wasn't much time, Abel needed to help the knight but more importantly, he need to help the knight without him finding out. After all, story tellers weren't allowed to interfere. He looked at his surroundings. There were barrels of explosives all in the tower...he could use it to explode the tower and make it fall on top of the dragon. If he could get the dragon to breath fire on it. With that Roderick had a chance to kill the beast before it recovered. He quickly opened a crate of black powder and quickly made a trail of it all the way down the tower till he was black in the plaza.

The knight and the dragon were now dancing around each other. Roderick avoiding the claws and stabbing at the dragon, the dragon merely being amused by his prey. Abel need to draw the attention of the dragon and Roderick. He picked up a stone and threw it at Roderick.

"Abel?! Get out of here, it's dangerous!" Roderick said in shock when he saw where Abel was standing. The dragon saw it too, he also saw a much easier lunch. The dragon lunged for Abel but before he could reach him Sir Roderick had jumped on his neck and was slashing his head from the back.

Abel ran away from where he was standing and the dragon in his anger fired a purple flame at him. The black powder ignited and 2 seconds later a loud explosion toppled the tower on the dragon and his rider. The dragon was dead.

Abel let out a breath as he sat down near a wall.
He had tried his best after all...he had tried to save the knight...
but it seemed it was for nothing...he wasn't a hero...he was
just a story teller. But he would write that this knight had not
died in vain. He had died a true hero.
"To Sir Roderick! The Knight in Shining Armor!" he toasted the
air.
"Awww, Abel...that is too kind of you," he heard Roderick's
voice.
"Sir Roderick?!" Able exclaimed. A rock was pushed away and
the knight appeared from under it.
"Help me out will ya," Roderick said smiling. Abel ran up to him
and pulled him out.
"I am so glad you are still alive," Abel said not quite believing
himself.
"And so am I," Roderick said. "Great work with the black
powder Abel," he said.
"I...I...well you weren't supposed to see that," Abel said
ashamed.
"Oh right, story tellers are not to interfere...well I don't care, I
am glad you did, you are a hero in my book!" Roderick said
smiling. "And that's what we are going to do, you are going to
stop writing about Sir Roderick and we will start writing the
book called: Abel and Roderick, story tellers in shining armor!
Well...after we clean this armor up a bit...it's full of dirt and
dragon remains...yuck,"
Abel laughed and Roderick started laughing too, they both
laughed till the sun was shining bright and then they walked
back to the village to start writing a new chapter of Abel and
Roderick, story tellers in shining armor.

Short story 15 – Hatius the Powerful

Supreme overlord Hatius the Powerful walked through the gates of his enormous stronghold. His men saluted them but he ignored them. He was angry. He quickly ascended the stairs to his main chamber and set down on his throne.
"Stressful day at work, H?" a female voice said to him. It was Fiz, a fairy light who had been by his side for most of his life. She was the only one who was allowed to call him H and only if no one else was around.
"Yeah...damn those heroes that always want to defeat me," he said angrily.
"Well...you are the Supreme overlord...heroes just do what they are meant to do, vanquish evil," Fiz suggested.
"Tell me something I don't know! But it gets boring being evil and supreme...you know, sometimes I wish I could be a hero," he said. Fiz laughed out loud.
"You?! A hero?!" Fiz laughed. "The only kindness you ever did was not killing me where I flew,"
"I know...I know...but you know...I could try it you know...you know, that's it, I am going to change myself into a hero, people will love me, you'll see!" Hiatus said resolutely and went to his magic lab. Fiz followed him.
"I'll need to change a bit of course, I can't have people recognize me and someone should stay here in my place," he said as he opened his spell book and started to mix potions in a pot.
"Fiz, I'm going to give you a gift and I hope you use it well. Betray me...and you'll know what happens," he said. With that he waved his hand and Fiz turned into an exact copy of Hatius.
"Wow...H, this is awesome...don't worry...I'll keep things going here," Fiz said smiling broadly. It looked weird on Hatius' face.

Hatius nodded and took a bowl in the potion he had created. "With this my magic will be limited and I will look human, it will also provide me with armor and weaponry," he explained to Fiz. He drank it up with a poof the Supreme overlord Hatius disappeared and a young blond haired, blue eyed man appeared wearing full armor and big sword around his belt.

"I am Atris," the man said.

"Yes, you are" Fiz said smiling again. "Now go, before someone sees you,"

Atris nodded using the limited magic he still possessed to teleport himself away. He was outside his own castle and looked upon it.

"When I get back...I should redecorate...its really gloomy," he nodded and went off in the other direction to find adventure and heroic deeds to complete.

He walked for four days and the sun was shining in the air and at night the moon was bright. He actually started to enjoy it and wondered why the sun was never shining in his kingdom.

He suddenly heard a scream of a woman. Almost overjoyed with himself he ran towards the sound and saw that the woman was being robbed by men in dark armor...his men...he never ordered his men to rob stuff...why would he?

He drew his sword and walked up to them.

"Leave that woman alone!" He shouted. The men turned around and laughed.

"Really? You are challenging us?" one of the men asked.

"You really should go play somewhere else," another man said.

"No, I think I'm just fine here," Atris said. He charged and not a minute later he was the last man standing. The woman stood up.

"Thank you," she said looking towards the dead bodies.

"You're welcome," Atris said smiling. He put his sword away.

"How can I ever repay you?" the woman said gathering her belongings from the floor.

"Your thanks is enough milady, also can you tell me if this happens a lot?" he asked kneeling down gathering some fruit that had fallen out of the bag.

"Only in the last couple of days...normally this overlord stays by himself...now it seems he is sending out all of his troops," she said shaking her head. "I wonder what changed..."

Atris looked in the direction of his kingdom.

"No idea..." he said. He focused his attention back on the woman. "You need any help getting home?" he asked.

"No but thank you, what is your name if I may ask?"

I'm Ha...Atris," he said.

"Atris...that's a nice name, it was nice meeting you Atris, hopefully our next encounter with less heavily armed evil minions," she jokingly said.

"It was nice meeting you too," he said. He bowed and turned around.

The next couple of days he ran all through the kingdom finding his men, HIS men doing heinous acts he never considered doing. All where he asked this only started when he had left his castle. Was this Fiz's doing? He couldn't believe it.

"I have to go back to my castle," he said He used his magic to teleport back but instead of teleporting in his castle he was teleported outside.

"What the..." he said. "A protection field?"

A protection field would block any magical way of entering the building but he hadn't put one up.

"Fiz...." He said. He quickly walked to the back of the castle where there was a secret entrance way he quickly entered.

"If think you can stop me from entering my castle than you are wrong," he said to himself. He quickly made his way up to his chambers, having to hide a couple of times for his own guards. Then after a long trek upstairs he finally reached the throne room. He opened the door and walked in to see that the room was now made of pure hideous gold. Sofas made of red velvet and diamond chandeliers and crystal glasses.

"Fiz!" he shouted. Fiz, looking like Hatius sat up from his throne.

"Well, well, well, if it isn't my old friend H...Atris," he said mockingly. "Like what I did to the place?"

Atris walked towards him.

"Fiz, whatever you got in your head, you have to stop now!"

"Stop? Why? All these years I have been your servant and now I finally got power, given to me by yourself! Why would I give that back now?" Fiz said. Atris jumped at him but Fiz simply waved his hand and Atris flew backwards.

"Uhuh, I make the rules now, not you," Fiz taunted. Atris stood up and moved towards him again. Not long after he was tossed back again. Somehow he had to stop this madness. Atris thought...the only thing he could play on was pride.

"Yes you are correct Fiz, you are more powerful than I am," he said to Fiz.

"Yes, indeed! Now come to me and kneel servant!" Fiz said holding out his hand. Atris did as he was told and kneeled. Fiz smiled.

"Excellent, you'll be my court wizard," Fiz said happy laying his hand on Atris shoulder. This was the moment Atris was waiting for. He grabbed the fake wizard hand and turned it around.

"Aaa...H....come on...let me go....I was just playing with you..." Fiz tried to defend himself.

"Remember when you told me I only showed kindness once?" Atris asked through bare teeth,"

Fiz nodded frantically,"

"Yes, when you let me live right, when you let me live…" Fiz said.

"I guess I'm not a hero after all," Atris said suddenly taking his sword out and stabbing the would be overlord. His Atris disguise fell of him as the crumpled body of Fiz fell on the ground. Atris looked like himself again, like Hatius. A deep sadness swelled inside of him, for a moment…just a small moment he had felt like a hero, when he rescued that woman. "I never got her name…" he suddenly realized. "I never got her name…" he sat down and with his head in hands for the first time in decades he cried.

Short story 16 – Rushed conclusions

"It should have been obvious a long time ago," Detective Marcus Landis said to his colleague. Detective Brandon Reyes. His colleague looked at him with a raised eyebrow.
"How so?"
Marcus bent down to the body of Brody Noah he just shot. A serial killer who after 8 murders was finally found by Marcus. He had hoped to arrest the man but he just wouldn't give up.
"I'll tell you later," Marcus said getting up. "Wait here for the posse, I'm going to see Miss Rush,"
"Whatever you say," Brandon said. He pulled his phone out of his pocket and started to make a call. Marcus quickly walked back to the abandoned warehouse. Inside he used his flash light to make sure he didn't trip over anything and to the manager's office. Inside a woman was sitting on a chair with her hands tied.
"Miss Rush, I'm Detective Marcus Landis, you are save now," he identified himself. She made a sound but clearly she had been gagged.
"I'm going to untie you," he said kindly. With a knife he quickly cut the binders. Her mouth was duct taped shut.
"Okay, this going to hurt Miss Rush," he said. She nodded. He quickly pulled on the edge of the duct tape.
"MOTHERFU!" she yelled only controlling her words at the last moment.
"Go ahead miss, believe me I heard worse," Marcus joked. She smiled softly. He smiled back.
"Are you alright miss? You have been through quite a lot, a psychologist of the department will be made available for you," he started to say his standard speech.
"I'm fine detective, thank you," she said getting up. She

rubbed her wrists.

"We still going to need your statement Miss Rush," he said.

"But that can wait till tomorrow,"

"So, did you get him?" Miss Rush asked.

"Yes, we did, he won't bother anyone else again," Marcus said. The posse had arrived and Miss Rush was escorted home. Marcus and Brandon made their way back to the station.

"Well, I'm glad that we can close this case," Brandon said sitting down and putting his legs on his desk.

"Yeah, definitely," Marcus said copying his colleagues moves. "Now just for the infinite paperwork," he sighed.

"Yeah yeah, in five minutes," Brandon said getting up and walking to the coffee machine. Marcus chuckled and sat straight booting up his computer. This was going to be a long night.

Marcus made his way home at 11 pm and opened the door.

"Honey, I'm home...oh wait, I'm not married," he said jokingly. He entered his apartment, put his coat on the hangar and went into the living room. He quickly got a beer from the fridge and set down in front of his TV. The evening news was reporting about the catching of the serial killer. He didn't really feel like watching it. He quickly finished his beer, turned off the TV and went to bed.

He had a weird dream. It was about the murderer. He woke up sweaty. He didn't feel that well and went to take a shower. Afterwards he felt better and put the dream out of his head. He went to work. Brandon was already there putting coffee on his desk.

"G'Morning sunshine," he said.

"G'morning, moonflower," Marcus replied.

"You look like you had a very bad night," Brandon said. Marcus thought he had hid it pretty well but apparently not.

"Just a weird dream about the case," he said. "But that's not important, what do we have for today?" he said looking at a new file on his desk.

"The chief wants to..." Brandon started saying but was suddenly interrupted by the phone. He picked it up. After a couple of seconds he put it down.

"There is a new murder...same M.O as Brody Noah you just shot," Brandon said eyes widening.

"A copycat?" Marcus said.

"What else can it be...the killer is dead, right?" Brandon said getting up. They both walked out.

Half an hour later they arrived at the murder scene. It was a grizzly sight to see, just like all the other murder victims.

"How can this be?" Marcus wondered. "We didn't leak any details to the press,"

Brandon nodded. "This is really weird...let's finish this quickly... we need to see if this copycat got anything wrong that can lead to him,"

"Him?"

"Well, statistically speaking..."

Marcus nodded. When they were back at the station they both started to study the imagery of the scene and compare them to that of the previous murders.

"This is incredible...I can't see any difference..." Brandon said.

"There must be...it must be a copycat," Hours later Marcus stood up.

"I'm done for today...see you tomorrow," he said. He went back home and went to bed immediately. He closed his eyes and suddenly heard a voice.

"Detective..."

He opened his eyes, he saw nothing.

"Hello?" he asked feeling stupid.

"Detective…" he suddenly recognized the voice.

"Brody?"

"Yes!" suddenly the image of Brody appeared in his room in the corner.

"This can't be real…"

"Detective…I have limited time…you must listen…" Brody said almost begging. Marcus noticed he was sweating.

"You had the wrong person…I am not the killer…but don't worry…I am not angry at you…my life consisted of enough crimes that death is a release," Brody said.

"But all the evidence points towards you…" Marcus said feeling ridiculous answering him…

"Yes…and no…there is another…" Brody said.

"What do you mean?" Marcus said.

"Make haste, Detective, find my real name and you'll find the real killer," Brody said and he disappeared.

Marcus didn't sleep anymore that night. Early in the morning he went to the office and started looking at Brody Noah.

"Find his real name…" he said to himself. Brandon came in.

"You're in early…bad night again?"

Marcus nodded.

"What's on your mind partner?" Brandon asked worriedly. Marcus looked to his partner considering to tell him that he saw Noah's ghost last night in his bed room. He decided not to to tell that.

"What if we were wrong? And Noah didn't do it…"

"All the evidence points to him being…"

"What if there was someone else to which the evidence could be linked? Which means Noah wasn't the killer and the real serial killer is still on the loose and that the murder of yesterday isn't a copycat but the same serial killer?"

"Do you have anyone in mind?"

"I think we need to look into Noah's past, I think we missed something," Marcus said.

"Whatever you say partner, it beats looking at pictures of murder scenes anyway," Brandon said. They opened the case file and used their database and even called in some connections to look into other databases. A search result came on screen and Marcus looked at it. Then looked at it again…

"No…fucking…way…" he said.

"What?!" Brandon said quickly also looking at the screen.

"No…fucking…way…" he repeated. They both got up and went out.

They walked up to a small apartment complex and drew their guns. They made their way to the upper floor to apartment. A single door was there. They both took one site. Marcus nodded.

"THIS IS THE POLICE! OPEN THE DOOR!" he shouted. No reaction. Brandon kicked in the door. They walked in and cleared the room. They walked into the kitchen which was also empty. They entered the bedroom. There was no bed. One figure was sitting in the center of the room.

"Miss Rush, you are under arrest for nine murders, please come along peacefully," Marcus said.

"Took you long enough detective…how did you find out?" Miss Rush said laughing hysterically.

"Your twin brother, Brody Noah…born as Noah Rush," Marcus said.

"How did you get him so far to take the blame?" Brandon asked.

"Little brother was suicidal, he wanted to be caught and shot, I just gave him the opportunity," she said.

"Well and now we are here and you got caught anyway," Marcus said walking towards her with cuffs out. She suddenly stood up and pointed a gun. Marcus heard three shots and she fell down on the floor. He looked behind him and saw Brandon aiming his gun at her.

"Thanks partner," he said. Suddenly Brody appeared in front of them.

"Thank you detectives, I can finally rest now," he said disappearing again.

Brandon's mouth opened wide.

"Did you just see that?" he asked Marcus.

"Saw what?" Marcus said deliberately. Brandon pointed in the direction but then got Marcus' drift.

"Eh, nothing…never mind…let's call it in shall we…let's get the fuck out of here too," he said.

"Excellent idea," Marcus said looking back one more time.

Short story 17 – Lift

"I never liked lifts," Marc said. "I don't have claustrophobia or anything but it is really not my cup of tea,"
Becca looked at him incredulous. "And how is that going to help in our situation?" she asked.
"It won't…but I thought it would be nice to have a conversation while we wait," Marc said sitting down. Tom sat next to him.
"That's the spirit," he said cheerfully. "I'm Tom,"
"Marc,"
"Becca," she said grudgingly. All three of them looked at the other two people on the other side of the lift. An older man and an older woman.
"Randall," the man said giving a friendly smile, "And this is my wife Susan," he said.
"Why don't you invite them to our home as well!" his wife snapped.
"Calm down dear, just making conversation," Randall said. Suddenly the speaker in the lift crackled.
"Eh…hello?" a male voice said. He sounded young.
"Yes, we're here!" Marc said standing up walking to the speaker.
"Yes…eh, I can see you on the camera," the voice said. "We are doing our best to get you out of there as soon as possible," he said.
"Good! Do you know how long this is going to take?!" Becca asked impatiently.
"No ETA yet," the voice said unsure. "Does, eh, does anyone need medical attention or anything else?"
"We are all okay here," Randall said.
"No we're not!" his wife interjected.

"Yes we are! Shut up old hag!" Randall said patting her back kindly. Apparently this was common between the two of them as his wife smiled.

"Eh okay…well, we are going to work on our end, if I have any news I will let you know," the voice said. The radio disconnected and Marc sat back down again. He pulled out his phone.

"Damnit…no internet…can't even update my Facebook complaining about the stupid lift company," he said putting his phone away.

"Good…we don't need to update everyone always," Becca said also sitting down.

"Oh god…you're not one of those Luddites are you?" Marc said. Tom chuckled.

"Oh of course not, I have Facebook and use it gladly but I don't go around posting that I'm stuck in traffic or a lift," she said.

"You kids and your smartphones…I'm glad I got a cellphone that can call but of course the moment I would need it it doesn't work…" Randall said.

"Yes…and when it works you never call me!" Susan said.

"We are always together woman! Why would I call you?!" he said. They both sat down. Tom chuckled again.

"So, while we are stuck here…what shall we do?" he said.

"I spy with my little eye…" Marc said.

"No! Anything but I spy!" Becca said.

"You're no fun," Marc mock complained. "Fine…why don't we just tell something about ourselves? We are stuck here anyway, I'd like to know what kind of people I'm stuck with,"

"Sounds good, I'll start," Tom said. "So I am Tom, 36 years old, married with one kid, she's 8 and I work as IT specialist for a big company in this city,"

Becca said up straight.

"Hi, I'm Becca, 28, single and I work as barista," she said,
talking in the tone of someone attending an AA meeting.
"I'm Marc, 31, also single," he said looking at Becca. "I'm a
writer, mostly for some websites but I dabble in writing
fiction," he said.
"Writer? Wow...I would guess your parents wouldn't have
encouraged that," Becca said.
"No...not really...well I do have a background in IT," he said.
"Okay Randall, your turn,"
Randall looked at his wife. "I'm Randall, 72 years old, I live in
this building with my lovely wife Susan, she's 33...with lots of
experience," he joked. "I used to be an engineer, she used to
be a nurse....lovely bedside manners,"
The radio crackled again.
"Eh hello?"
"Yes," they all said in unison.
"We have discovered the problem but it will take some time to
fix it,"
"Well, at least you know what to fix, so that's something!"
Marc said.
"Eh...indeed...there might be some noise or movement in the
lift while we fix this, don't be afraid...nothing can go wrong,"
"Okay..." Tom said. The radio turned off.
"Did I mention I hate lifts?" Marc said.
"Yes, yes you did," the others said in unison.
"Good...because I really don't," he said.
"Then why did you get into this one?" Becca asked.
"Lady...I had to be on the 36th floor, do you really think I would
take the stairs for that?" he said.
Suddenly a loud bang was heard. They all jumped up as the
light went off for a second.
"What the..." Becca yelled.

"Take it easy," Marc said. "The voice said this could hap…"
Suddenly the lift moved and it felt like they were going down.
They screamed and Randall and Susan held each other firmly.
By lack of significant other Tom, Marc and Becca also held
each other. Then suddenly it stopped. Marc staggered to the
radio.
"Yo! Dude! Come on!" he yelled.
"Eh…yes?" the voice said.
"What the fuck was that?!"
"Ehm…I did tell you that the lift could move right…pretty sure I
did…yes…here it is on my paper… "told people lift could move"
See?"
"Yes…you did tell us that…but not 20 floors!"
"Technically only 17…and a half…" the voice said.
"That's beside the point! What's your name?" Marc asked.
"Why do you want to know?" the voice asked.
"I just like to know who I am talking too, if I'm going to be
stuck here for a couple more hours,"
"Well…ehm, let's hope it doesn't come to that…" the voice
said. "But my name is Matt," he said.
"Okay, Matt, nice meeting you, the name's Marc,"
"Yes…I knew that…we can hear and see everything on the
camera," he said. "Yes, that too Becca," he said. Becca put her
middle finger back down.
"So, any estimates yet?" Randall asked.
"Not yet…I will get back to y…" the lift suddenly moved again,
the light flickered and suddenly it stopped.
"Matt! What the fuck is happening!" Marc shouted.
"No worries, no worries," Matt said.
"Don't give me that! Tell me what is happening,"
"We are fixing it, calm down, we are fix…" the lift suddenly
started to go up with great speed. Marc fell down on the

ground.

"We are going to die aren't we…" Becca said softly.

"Not on my watch," Marc said getting up again. The lift suddenly stopped and Marc fell down again.

"Okay…now that's enough, Matt you better tell us what's happening or I swear to God I'm going to pull you right through that radio!"

"Ehm…that's not possible…I'm not literally in the radio…"

"Maatttt!" Marc said jumping up and smashing the camera.

"Now, you should not have done that Marc," Matt said, suddenly changing his tone and talking more seriously.

"And why shouldn't I have done that?" Marc said angry.

"Because now people can't watch you fall," Matt said. The lift suddenly started to move again. Becca crawled to Marc and whispered.

"What is going on?"

"Well…a wild guess but I think "Matt" here is the one who is causing this for some kind of sadistic purpose" Marc whispered back. Tom was thrown to a corner. Marc turned his head towards Randall and Susan…they were also laying on the floor.

"You okay?" he mouthed. Randall nodded. Marc crawled toward them while the lift changed from going down to up again.

"Randall, you were an engineer, any ideas…" Marc whispered. Matt interrupted them: "I don't know what you are talking about but don't think you can escape, you're mine! Mine!"

"Randall?"

"We need to find a way to cut the power…no power…he can't move the elevator and we need to cut it at a floor so we can open the door," Randall said.

"Okay…so…where would the power be?"

"There is a panel where Tom is...open it and you can cut the power...opening it...might be a problem," Randall said. Marc nodded. He crawled toward Tom.

"We need to open the panel beneath you, any idea..." Marc whispered.

"I got some tools in my bag...I was about to go to my uncle to fix his computer...there should be a screwdriver," Tom said. He sounded scared but resolute. Marc nodded and opened Tom's bag. He found the tools and the screw driver. Tom moved over and Marc started unscrewing the panel.

"Why is there always a panel?" Marc wondered. He opened it. There was a thick cable running through it.

"Okay...now cutting it without electrocuting myself," he said to himself.

"Here," Becca said, handing him some pink rubber gloves. "Why do you?"

"I sometimes work as a house keeper as a second job," Becca said getting a bit red.

"Nothing to be ashamed about," Marc said smiling. He put the gloves on and from his pocket he produced a Swiss army knife. He opened the knife and placed it against the cable.

"Randall, give me a sign" he said. Randall nodded. The waited and suddenly Randall said: "Now!"

Marc cut the cable and it went totally dark in the lift. Suddenly the lift door opened.

"Why did you destroy the camera Marc?" a familiar voice sounded in the dark. It was not through the speaker though. It was right here in the elevator. A flash light was turned on and the silhouette of a man appeared.

Then suddenly a fist from the right side knocked the man on the ground.

"Susan!" Randall shouted.

"Good work Susan!" Tom said.

"Amazing!" Marc and Becca said. They all got out of the elevator leaving the man on the floor there.

"Okay, let's go to our apartment and call the police," Randall said. The five of them walked towards the apartment and called the police. They waited there while the police arrested Matt and questioned them. It was getting late at night and they all started to make their way home.

Marc turned to walk to the staircase when Becca hurried behind him.

"Hey...wanna add me on Facebook?" she asked.

"What, so we can share the story on how we were stuck in the lift together?" he joked.

"That...and maybe more..." she said. Marc laughed and together they took the stairs down to the exit.

Short story 18 – Three may keep a secret

Three may keep a secret, if two of them are dead – Benjamin Franklin

"Don't you hate it when movies or tv shows start with a vague quote that somehow relates to the story in a very intangible way? I do. Especially when it's misused," Mick said taking a sip from his coffee.
"Why do you care so much about that?" Ron said laughing looking at his best friend. "Do you believe this guy Amy?"
"Well, he has a point…I remember seeing lots of movies with so called famous quotes from Mark Twain for example and then it wasn't even mentioned in the story itself, what a bunch of pretentious bullshit that is!" she exclaimed.
"You two have way too much time on your hands that you are worrying about that!" Ron said. "Meanwhile here in the real world we have this project to finish,"
"Yeah yeah…so what do we have so far?" Mick said waving the waitress over.
"The title, oh and lots of data that we need to filter out," Ron said showing them the screen of his laptop.
"Hmmm, yes…it seems we still have some work today, we are going to need a lot more coffee!" Mick said. The waitress just came to their side.
"So, three more coffee then?" she asked.
"Let's start with three," Amy said. "But probably more later,"
The waitress nodded and walked away. Amy opened her laptop as well as did Mick.
"Okay, we'll be sifting through the data, you start working on writing it all down,"
The next couple of hours they worked in silence, only

sometimes commenting on interesting little bits of data and ordering more coffee or taking a short break. In the evening they decided that they should leave it for today and continue tomorrow. Which was good anyway as the cafe was closing. They went outside and stepped into Mick's car. Ron and Amy set in the back.

"Now, keep your hands of each other back there, I don't want to get my car dirty!" Mick joked as he started to drive. He turned on some "Uptown Funk". He heard some giggling on the back ground.

"Guys! Wait till your home!" he said. They were driving on a dark road now in the middle of nowhere. Ron and Amy were clearly in their own world when suddenly Mick felt a sharp pain on his shoulder and turned the wheel hearing a loud bang. He quickly slammed the break.

"Guys!" Mick yelled.

"Woah...what happened?!" Ron asked.

"I think I hit something! That's what happened!" Mick said frustrated. More from the shock than anything else. He unbuckled his seat belt and went outside. Ron and Amy followed him, still buttoning up their shirts. Mick walked to the front of his car and suddenly stood still.

"Oh no..." he said.

"What?" Amy asked standing next to him looking down. Her mouth fell open.

Ron also stood next to them now. "Oh god..."

In front of the car not moving was a young woman, the waitress of the cafe they were all day. Mick knelt down and checked her pulse. He couldn't feel anything.

"She's..." He couldn't finish the sentence.

"Oh no, oh no, oh no," Amy shouted, she started to jump around.

"Relax!" Ron shouted.

"Relax? Relax?! A woman just died and you tell us to relax?!" Mick yelled.

"Yes, relax, it was an accident, we couldn't help it, she just showed up..." Ron started.

"As if they will fall for that...we are doomed..." Amy said, she started to cry.

"Well...maybe..." Ron said.

"Maybe?!" Mick said.

"Yeah...I mean...we are the only ones here...the car is alright, we can just leave and nobody would be the wiser, we are the only ones who would know.

"We can't do that...that's unethical..." Mick said not believing what he's hearing.

"I think Ron's right..." Amy said. "We all agree it was an accident and that we could not have done something about it...then why should we suffer for it?"

Mick shook his head. "I can't believe you are saying this...you really want to leave her here and pretend it didn't happen?" he asked looking at his friends.

"We have to, we are too young to have our lives ruined...you wouldn't want that right?" Ron said pleading. Mick slowly nodded.

"Okay...okay...let's get out of here..." he said reluctantly. They got back into the car and quickly drove home without saying a word. He dropped his friends of at their house.

"And remember, only three of us know...we can keep a secret right?" Ron asked.

"Yeah yeah, got it..." Mick said. He drove away to his own home. He parked the car in the garage and checked the front for damages. It looked fine, nobody would ever know what happened on that road.

The next morning he woke up because his phone was ringing.
"Yo," he said as he picked up.
"It's Ron, you better check the news," he said and hung up. On the news was the report of the woman being found on the road and a call of the police to help finding who did it. Immediately his stomach turned.
He suddenly realized something that hadn't occurred to him last night. He was the driver so if someone would be blamed for this it would be him. Even though he lost control of the car because of Amy's foot they still would blame him.
So, he was not protecting them, they were protecting him and for what price? He thought back at how quickly Ron and Amy had decided to leave the woman and pretend it didn't happen. Would they do the same with him? Deciding to leave him rotting in jail or letting him die if it was convenient for them?
"No, no...don't be ridiculous," he said to himself. But the thought kept nagging at him and he realized there were only two solutions. One go to the police and get arrested and have his whole life ruined and two...
He didn't want to think of solution two but he knew it had to be done. He called his friends to check if they were still going to meet up at the cafe as it would look weird if they suddenly didn't. Ron agreed and asked if he could pick them up. Mick was going to suggest exactly the same. An hour later he picked them up and went to the cafe. They had to go a different route as the road was closed, probably because the police was still investigating. They arrived at the cafe to see it was closed because of private reasons. Mick felt his stomach getting heavy again. They went to another coffee shop not far from there and set down with their laptops. It was difficult to stay focused on working on the project, he noticed that Ron and Amy were also constantly exchanging glances and the normal

fun time chatter was an absolute low.

They worked for straight 8 hours and got a surprisingly a lot of work then. When they stepped out of the coffee shop they laughed.

"Wow…almost done with the project, good work guys," Ron said being his cheerful self again.

"Yeah, one more day and we should be finished," Mick said also smiling.

"Good…because this whole project is really tiring me out," Amy said. They stepped into the car. They both sat in the back again.

"Guys, be a little more careful today okay?" Mick joked.

"Yeah yeah…" Ron said impatiently. Mick started to drive, they went the same way home as the day before. The police had finished their investigation and the road was open again. Mick heard lots of giggling from the back seats again and rolled his eyes. He looked between his legs were he had put a heavy rock. With a bit of difficulty he put the rock on the gas pedal. It worked, the car was now going by itself without him having to press the gas.

"Say guys, if our life was a movie, what kind of beginning quote would you think it would have?" He asked.

Ron stuck his head between the seats.

"Dude…we are kinda busy here…ehm…how about: Shut up when people are busy," Ron said annoyed and went back to whatever he was doing with Amy.

"Nice…very nice…" Mick said. There was a sharp turn he had to take in about a 100 meters otherwise the car would fall down about 50 meters. He used some plastic tubes he also had with them to fixate the wheel so it would go straight.

"I was thinking more in the line of the great Benjamin Franklin," he said.

"What did he say?" Amy asked giggling not really paying attention.
"Three may keep a secret, if two of them are dead"
Ron and Amy both sat up right. Mick opened the door and jumped out. The last words he heard were from Ron:
"You bastard!"
The car went straight through the barrier in the corner and down the hill. Mick didn't even go to look. He turned around and walked the long way back home.

Short story 19 – And he lived happily ever after

"Those movies gives as such a bad name," Yuri said in a thick Romanian accent.
"Well, I'm sure the blood sucking doesn't really help…" Christopher said.
"Well, I guess…but do you judge a lion because it eats gazelles?" Yuri answered. Christopher laughed.
"Not really the same thing Yuri, you eat humans…well their blood anyway, if you'd stick to cows or rats I'm sure people would be less upset,"
"Ugh…rats…are you fucking kidding me? I have standards you know," Yuri said mock severely.
"Aha! So you have eaten rats!" Christopher said laughing again. He enjoyed these little chats with his new immortal friend. They met each other just a week ago. Christopher was about to kill himself when Yuri stopped him. He guessed that Yuri felt some pity for him. He could have killed him then and there but somehow he didn't. Christopher was happy he didn't. Yuri had opened his eyes about a whole new world. A world where vampires existed and who knows what more.
"So, are you going to change me into a vampire?" he asked not for the first time.
"You know I can't…there are rules…even us talking about this is breaking a few of them actually," Yuri said sounded remorseful.
"But why? Can't every vampire do this?" Chris asked.
"Technically yes but there is this thing called "The masquerade", it's like a holy rule book.
"I heard about…in some video game called: Vampire: The Masquerade, I used to watch videos of a guy playing the game on YouTube but he never finished it,"

"Yes, I know of the game…scarily accurate…I think someone from us had some influence…I wonder if our government had it investigated…either way…there are rules about who gets to be a vampire or not. If I make you a vampire they will surely kills us both," Yuri said.

"It's not fair, you save my life, show me this whole new world and then tell me I can't be part of it," Christopher said.

"I am truly sorry," Yuri said. He checked his watch. "I need to go, same time tomorrow?"

"I'll be here," Christopher said. It was 4 am and he still had some time to sleep before he had to go to work. Yuri had already disappeared. Probably using some kind of vampire trick to turn invisible or run fast. Christopher felt insanely jealous.

He went home and slept for a couple of hours. It was day when he woke up. He drank a full pot of coffee and then went to his dead end job in a dead end factory and was feeling even more depressed then a week ago. He got home, eat a pizza and waited. Waited for night to fall so he could visit his friend, his only friend.

It was almost twelve o'clock. Christopher went outside and to their meeting spot. Yuri should show up soon. Normally he would have already eaten. Both for Christopher's safety and also because it was much more fun to talk if he wasn't hungry. Christopher waited for an hour but Yuri didn't show up. That was weird, normally he would already be there. He had no way to contact Yuri, no phone number or Facebook or whatsapp. Christopher started to panic.

"Calm down, Chris," he said to himself breathing deeply. He was thinking back to all the conversations they had and he suddenly remembered that Yuri had mentioned a place where he would go often.

"A warehouse...on the other side of the city...at the docks" he
said to himself...already regretting the thought of getting there
but he had too, his friend might be in danger and that was his
only lead. He went to the bus stop and saw he was in luck,
even at this late hour there would be a bus soon. About fifteen
minutes later he stepped into the empty bus.
"I want to go to the docks," he said.
"At this hour? Why would you want to go there now?" the bus
driver asked surprised.
"My...my...I work there and forgot my bag," he made up...not
sure why he was even bothering with lying, maybe just in case
somebody asked.
"Suit yourself," the driver said accepting the money. During the
45 minute trip the driver only had to stop a couple of times
but as soon as he was reaching the docks the bus was empty.
"Here we are sonny," he said opening the door. "Now, I know
it's none of my business but the last bus out of here is in 45
minutes so you better be back then...it's dangerous out here at
night,"
"I know...thank you," Christopher said. He got out of the bus
and put up his hood.
"A warehouse at the docks...well luckily there aren't much of
those," he said sarcastically. He looked around not sure where
to go and then decided to climb somewhere higher and see if
he could see some light somewhere, although he was pretty
sure that vampires could see in the dark. He climbed up the
roof of a building and saw exactly one warehouse where a
light was burning in the window.
"Well...it's a long shot..." he said, climbing down and making
his way towards the building. Not only was there light there
was lots of activity inside as well. He could hear talking and
also some noise which sounded like knocking. He made his

way to a window and looked inside. What he saw there shocked him for life. Yuri was sitting shirtless in a chair, his hands were tied. There were cuts and bruises all over his body. Another man, a vampire, he assumed was standing in front of him. The window was open and he could hear him speak.
"You broke too many rules Yuri," the leader said. "Hanging around with a human, telling him our secrets is just the latest in your long list of crimes," he continued, marking the end of a sentence with a punch.
"Aaah, but I see that you trained the human well, he's here now," he said looking directly at Christopher. "Bring him!" Christopher turned around to run but before he could move one of the other vampires who was just in the room was standing in front of him. Not much later he was also tied to a chair and sitting next to Yuri.
"Hi Yuri," Christopher said.
"Hey," Yuri said smiling a bit.
"I was wondering why you didn't show up,"
"Ah well, you know...tied up in business as usual," Yuri joked.
"Silence!" the leader said.
The leader looked at Christopher and then at Yuri.
"You are not afraid?" he asked.
"Of you? No...the only thing you can do to me is kill me and I was willing to do that myself last week," Christopher said.
"Ooh, very brave...but I can make it very painful," the leader said.
"Doesn't matter if the end result is still the same," Christopher said. The leader smacked him in his face.
"Silence human!"
His phone suddenly rang and he picked up.
"Yes?" he listened then waved his hand and he and his guards disappeared into a different room.

Yuri turned to him.

"Quick…we need to get out…I don't have the strength to do it by myself…but I can give you the strength you need,"

"But that's forbidden!" Christopher said.

"As if these guys care about the legality of things, they are just pissed of that I don't want to deal with them, now bite me in my wrist," he said.

"How do you suppose I do that…" he said shrugging to show him he was stuck.

"We fall over and scoot to each other," Yuri sighed rocking his chair sideways till he fell. Christopher did the same.

"This better not be a a hidden cam show," Christopher said. With difficulty he moved over to the wrists of Yuri.

"Okay…the idea is that you drink my blood, this will change you into a vampire, the process is pretty quickly luckily," Christopher sighed, this was not going to be pretty.

"Just get it over with," Yuri said. Christopher bit and drank the blood of his friend. He immediately felt stronger and broke the rope around his wrists.

"Wow…this is amazing,"

"Yeah yeah, they're all amazed till the killing and bloodsucking starts….get me out of here will you!" he said impatiently. Christopher smiled as he untied his friend.

"Good, now let's get out…"

"They're free!" Christopher heard the leader shout.

"You need to fight them!" Yuri said breaking of a leg of the chair. "Take this, stab them in the heart quickly before they expect it,"

Christopher nodded. He moved to the two body guards quickly and disposed of them with a super quick stab to the heart. He then turned around to the leader who had Yuri in a grip.

"Let him go!" Christopher shouted. Yuri shook his head.

"Get out of here Chris! Live!" he shouted. Suddenly a dark red mark appeared on the chest of Yuri as he fell dead on the ground with another wooden chair leg sticking out of his back. "You!" Christopher said moving towards the leader with such anger and fervor that the leader didn't expect it. He was dead before he could even get a word out. Christopher looked back at his friend and then went outside. It was getting late...or early...and he needed to get out of the sun.

"It isn't fair...now I finally got what I wanted and now my only friend died..." he said to himself crying. Maybe I should just stay till the sun comes...end it all to day. Then he remembered the last words of his friend.

"Get out of here Chris! Live!"

He would honor his friends' last wish, to live. He ran home quicker than he had ever ran before. Because the next night he would live! He would live like he had never lived before! And he would do this till eternity! He had a purpose now and for the first time in a long long time he felt genuinely happy.

Shorty story 20 – It was purple but darker

"Let's try something different," the old man named Richard said looking at his young grandson who was floating in a tube with a liquid inside. The boy was wearing a breathing mask but had his eyes closed and didn't seem to hear the man.
"Log entry #726 – Test subject was non responsive to external stimuli with previous formula, going to adjust formula and try again in 12 hours," the man said into his recording device. He put it down and sighed.
"I'm so sorry Nick...we will try again tomorrow okay?" he said to the boy. The old man got up from his chair and walked to the stairs using his cane to support him. He realized that he didn't have much time left. He put the thought out of his mind and went upstairs.
There was a lovely smell coming from the kitchen and he smiled. His wife had made meatballs again. His favorite.
"Ah, there you are! I was just about to come downstairs," she said smiling walking out of the kitchen. "Dinner is ready," she said.
"I noticed," he smiled back licking his lips. He followed her to the dining room. Their house was not super big but there was separate dining room, two bedrooms upstairs and of course a large basement where he had built a laboratory, ever since he stopped working for the university he had spent his time there in his lab trying to find a cure for his grandson. He felt it was the last thing he could do to honor the memory of his late daughter and son-in-law who died in the same car accident which put his grandson in his current condition.
Considered brain dead by all doctors he had opted for taking his grandson home and have him there die in peace. Instead he wanted to cure his grandson. Not entirely legal of course so

that's why only he and his wife knew. She didn't agree at first but as her grandson was the only living family member she still got (aside from him of course) she reluctantly agreed. Officially he had died and he was "buried" next to his parents on a cemetery not far from here. The man had retired and used his well-earned money to build a laboratory and started to study. This was almost ten years ago.

Richard felt old. He knew his days were numbered and he felt like he wasn't getting closer to a solution. His wife, Martha, had of course noted.

"No success today?" she asked, knowing the answer.

"No...and I'm running out of options...and time..." he said morosely.

"Now now, dear, I'm sure you still have enough of either," she said giving him a soft smile. "But first, eat," she said resolutely. He nodded and started to eat. Like always it tasted like heaven. They were watching television while his mind was still on his grandson. Somehow he had to find a solution, a way to make this work. He owed it to his daughter, herself also quite a brilliant scientist before her life was taken. That gave him an idea.

"Martha...do we still have the papers Denise was working on?" he asked.

"Of course we do...they should be up the attic, why?" she asked.

"Maybe...just maybe she has the solution I'm looking for, her work as a neuroscientist was pretty ground breaking," he said. He stood up, got his cane and walked upstairs. The third staircase had him pretty winded when he finally reached the attic. It was dusty there, no one really came up here. The cleaning lady only did the first and second floor, the basement was his domain so the attic mostly stayed dirty and dusty. In the middle of the room stood a single chair and lots of boxes with Denise and Rick's old stuff. He searched through the box of academic papers that Denise had written throughout her career and opened a particularly interesting one.

He didn't bother to go downstairs now, he was reading the paper and suddenly closed it.

"Yes! This is it! This is what I need!" he said enthusiastically. He walked downstairs, carefully of course. Martha was just coming up.

"Are you alright dear?" she asked looking worried.

"Yes, I'm fantastic! Denise has solved the puzzle! I know how to get Nick better now!" he said. His wife smiled cautiously, this wasn't the first time.

"That's fantastic news Richard,' she said.

"It is! And I wish I could implement it right now but I need some extra stuff from the shop...so that will have to wait till tomorrow I guess..." he said slightly disappointed.

"Yes indeed, so now...let's go to sleep," she said. Richard nodded knowing he would hardly get any sleep tonight.

The next morning he had discovered that he was right. He stretched and got up with great difficulty. His muscles hurt. His wife had already gone downstairs, preparing breakfast from the smell of it.

He went down and quickly had breakfast, then he went out to the hardware store. Not soon afterwards he got back with the stuff that he needed. He went down and spent all day building his new prototype that would stimulate the nerves of the brains directly, together with his formula this should work.

"It will work, it will" he said to himself. It was already starting to be late but he absolutely wanted to finish it today. Martha came down and saw her husband working hard. She realized that he would never come up for food now so she left him. It

was nice to see him so happy again.
A couple hours later he had finished.
"Log entry #727 – Starting test now. Activating Neuron...activator...wow I need a better name for this."
He pressed a button and a soft whirring could be heard.
"Applying formula" he continued.
Nothing seemed to happen. Disappointed he shut down the machine and looked at his grandson. He looked away and then looked back. His eyes were open!
"Nick?"
The boy got a look of recognition in his eyes.
"Nick!" the old man exclaimed.
"Martha! Martha! Come down! Nick's alive! He's alive!"
His wife came down to her husbands yelling and immediately started to cry when she saw her grandson.
"It's a miracle!" she shouted and hugged her husband.
"It's okay Nick, we'll get you out of there, we just need to run a few more tests to make sure we can," Richard said smiling a reassuring smile. The little boy nodded.
"We have so much to tell you but for now, please relax," he continued. He checked his computer and all the values seemed to be good.
"I'm going to lower the water now," he said. Martha had gone upstairs to get some clothes and a towel and was coming back as the water was drained from the tank. Nick was sitting on the ground unable to move.
"You haven't used your muscles for some time now, just take it easy," Richard said. Martha wrapped the towel around the boy.
"Where...where...is...mama?" the boy said with difficulty, he also hadn't use his voice for some time now.
"Well...that's a difficult question...but you deserve to know the

truth...your mother, father and you were in an accident...a fatal accident...do you understand me?"
Nick understood alright. With an energy that came out of nowhere he stood up and started kicking stuff around crying his eyes out.
"What happened to me?!" he shouted.
"You were...in a coma of sorts...I spent the last 10 years trying to heal you," Richard said a bit worried.
Suddenly Nick was quiet again looking at his grandpa and smiling.
"Thank you grandpa," he said running towards him and hugging him.
"That's alright, son," Richard said lifting him up. "Let's get you out of this lab and into a bedroom.
All three of them went upstairs and Richard brought Nick to the second bedroom he had prepared for this.

"Okay, for now you need to rest, I will have some things here that will monitor your health but if everything goes well then tomorrow we are going to work to get you back to perfect health," Richard explained calmly. Nick nodded suddenly looking very tired. He went to sleep.
Richard went to the master bedroom where he had put the equipment to monitor his grandson.
"He'll be fine Richard," Martha said.
"I know," Richard said.
The next day Richard went to his grandson to find him already awake.
"How are you feeling?" he asked, unplugging the monitors.
"Very good grandpa," Nick said. Then he wrinkled his forehead, just like his mother, when he was trying to remember something.

"I think I remember something of the accident," he said.
"Owww...you don't have to think about those things right now..." Richard said.
"It's not really up to me to what I remember right?" the boy asked. Richard nodded reluctantly in agreement.
"I was talking to mom, about a book I had read...I said it had a purple cover...I said it was purple but darker, then she said: Ah, like dark purple? And then mom and dad started to laugh...I don't know why...and then everything went dark..." Nick finished, realizing he was crying.
"It's okay son, it's okay," Richard said. He brought Nick downstairs and they had breakfast. Nick seemed to be completely back to his old self. Everything seemed to be completely fine.
It was a week after the experiment that Richard noticed that Nick was losing hair. When he woke up his grandson some hair stayed behind. Also he noticed that Nick seemed to be getting thinner.
He decided to run a blood test that day and the results weren't what he had hoped for.
He went to his grandson's bedroom where the boy was playing a video game. He saw his grandfather ad the worried look on his face.
"I'm going to die again am I not?" Nick said looking him straight in the eyes.
"Yes...I'm so sorry...there is nothing I can do...you only have a few days left..." he said starting to cry.
"It's okay grandpa, you gave me this wonderful week. I could not have asked for more," he said.
"You are quite wise for a 10 year old," Richard said.
"Well, technically I'm twenty," he replied.
"Nobody likes a smart-ass you know," Richard said laughing

through the tears.
The next few days Nick slowly was getting worse and worse. He stayed in his bed and read a lot. On one night Richard and Martha were sitting next to his bed and he was barely awake.
"Grandpa...I was reading a book the other day...but I cannot remember it," he said.
"Can you describe it? Maybe I can find it," Richard said softly.
"It was purple...but darker," he said. Richard smiled softly.
"Ah, like dark purple?"
"Exactly" Nick said smiling and closing his eyes for the final time.

www.ingramcontent.com/pod-product-compliance
Lightning Source LLC
Chambersburg PA
CBHW071913120726
48001CB00005B/1729